Dear Reader:

When Rita Clay Estrada sent us *The Ivory Key*, we were in a quandary. A completely satisfying romance from beginning to end, it was warm, sensuous and irresistibly readable. In so many ways it was a perfect Temptation.

But. . . this story had one extraordinary element we'd never seen in a romance. Would our readers go for it? Each of *us* had read Hope and Armand's story with laughter and tears . . . and shivers down our spines. That's why we finally decided to bring you *The Ivory Key*. We'd love to hear *your* reaction to this very special book.

Rita Clay Estrada always strives to make her romance novels believable. She has succeeded admirably in the more than a dozen books she's written. Not one to rest on her laurels, though, Rita challenged herself to write the ultimate love story... with the ultimate conflict. The result? *The Ivory Key*, a contemporary romance with a big difference.

In her dual role of author and homemaker, Rita often has a hectic schedule. When she isn't writing or being interviewed about writing, Rita dedicates her time to her family. She, her husband and their four children live in Texas.

Books by Rita Clay Estrada

HARLEQUIN TEMPTATION

The Ivory Key

RITA CLAY ESTRADA

Harlequin Books

TORONTO • NEW YORK • LONDON
AMSTERDAM • PARIS • SYDNEY • HAMBURG
STOCKHOLM • ATHENS • TOKYO • MILAN

This book belongs to many:

To two good friends, Pat and Bob Thompson, whose love of Minnesota's arrowhead area inspired the location.

To Anita Solomon, who played devil's advocate and allowed me to bounce my ideas off her.

To Birgit Davis-Todd, who patiently worked with me to create Hope and Armand's story.

And to Star Helmer, who bought this crazy premise to begin with!

Thank you, all.

Published August 1987

ISBN 0-373-25266-8

1

Someone was watching her.

Hope Langston sat on the crest of the small hill and
stared out at the shimmering blue Minnesota lake while
almost silent waves lapped the shore of Teardrop
Island. Peaceful, partially forested terrain surrounded
her. She should have been relaxed and content, absorbing the barely tamed wilderness. Instead her whole
body had become rigid, the small hairs at the base of
her slim neck bristling like starched cat fur. Someone
was watching her again. She knew it. She could feel it.

Carefully Hope lowered her camera to the bed of soft
moss next to her. She leaned casually against the coarse-
barked pine trunk and stared at the water coursing
slowly around her tiny island. Birds chirped in the trees,
flitting gaily from limb to limb, stopping only briefly
to exchange chatter. The warm summer breeze caressed her cheek, touched her hair and then moved on.
Hope ignored it all, her concentration elsewhere. Her
heartbeat was a heavy thud within the constriction of
her rib cage. The breath wheezed through her throat
short and fast.

Someone was watching her. She was sure of it.

She turned her head quickly, dark brown eyes darting through the webbed green foliage of the trees, stopping at shadows and at leaves stirred by the breeze.
Nothing had changed. A large boulder was just to her

left. It grew out of the ground as if it had been one of the first things God planted the day he made the rich, brown earth. Late-afternoon sun made the rock's shadow resemble a giant eggplant, and Hope chuckled nervously at that thought. That must be it. She was still spooked from her recent experiences.

Both her father and her boss had been right. She desperately needed a vacation, away from everything that reminded her of that nasty little Central American country whose policy was to kidnap the wealthy, torture them and apologize later. Two months in their idea of jail should have been enough to kill her, but she had been lucky and lived through it . . . barely.

As her father's closest relative, she should have taken better precautions. He headed an American oil company based in Central America, and the politics there were in constant turmoil. She was just damn lucky she had lived. Other prisoners hadn't.

Hope picked up her camera and fiddled with the controls, aimed it toward the giant-sized rock and clicked; then she focused on the surrounding woods, the shadow, the tops of the trees and the edge of the small path that led off the crest of the hill and to the shore below. There was nothing there but the scenery.

Her brain, usually so alert, was playing tricks on her, and she was falling for them. Every time she had ever sat on this particular spot, the highest and widest on the ten-acre island, the strong sensation of being closely observed had come over her. When she was little, after her parents' divorce, she and her mother had vacationed here during the summer. Then she had loved the feeling that someone was monitoring her actions, as though God was looking benevolently over her shoulder. She had been a lonely child, and it had given her peace. As an adult it was an unusual feeling, but one that vanished quickly when she left the small hilltop.

Sunset began its beautiful, heart-stopping show, turning the day into night. Dark shadows formed and merged to produce even larger, more sinister shapes of gray. The mournful, laughing call of a loon echoed across the water.

Slowly Hope descended the hill and angled toward the old white two-storied farmhouse, relaxing as she walked along. The house had been here for over fifty years. Originally it had belonged to a fisherman and his family, but rumor had it they had done more truck farming in the field behind the house than commercial fishing in the lake.

She marveled that she felt more comfortable on the island, isolated and alone, than she ever had anywhere else. Even when she thought she was being watched, she knew whoever it was wasn't hostile or angry. Perhaps curious, sometimes caring . . . occasionally loving.

No, that didn't make any sense. How could someone, especially someone around here, love her, when she didn't know anyone who cared two figs or a camera filter for her? Her imagination had truly gone haywire.

Dinner was a bland affair: a frozen dinner of chicken breasts on toast, smothered with cream gravy and instant mashed potatoes the consistency of melted whipped cream. At least it was an attempt at a balanced diet, something that had been missing from her life for the past several months. She fortified herself with one of the many vitamin pills her doctor had prescribed. As she did, she looked out the kitchen window toward the small knoll beyond, debating whether or not to develop the film she'd exposed that afternoon. Why not? She didn't have anything better to do, and the familiar routine would be soothing.

Hope's darkroom equipment was set up in one of the closets. On other stays here, when her mother was still alive, she had never visited long enough to establish her own working area. Now she was in residence for the rest of the summer and the fall—or for as long as it took to get herself back into shape after being held hostage.

She slipped a Paul Horn cassette into the player, fidgeted with the speaker balance until she was satisfied, then reached for her camera, automatically rewinding the film as she headed for the stairs. It would be fun to see if there were any photos worth selling to one of the many magazines who'd purchased her work before. It was a game to her, one that she had played often.

Right after graduating from college, she had acquired a camera, finding an affinity with it that she had never known with anything before. Since then, she had carried it everywhere, and it had become her entrée into places that nice young women usually didn't go. Her subjects always thought she was a professional. It had worked so well that in no time photography had developed into a career. Whenever she was at a political affair, her camera focused and shot while she took mental notes, her mind clicking right along with her camera. The politicos hadn't seemed to mind enough to stop talking because they had never seen her with a pencil in her hand.

Still, she was surprised how often a shot she had thought was ordinary when she clicked it turned out to be terrific. A few of them had sold for top dollar. Some were hanging on the farmhouse walls, along with the framed awards they had earned. A few more hung in the headquarters of *Today's World*, the magazine she now worked for exclusively. Well, almost exclusively. She still free-lanced for others occasionally.

But at *Today's World* she also wrote copy. Exciting and fulfilling, the dual role gave her the best of both worlds. She could document a scene with her camera and fill in what she couldn't see with what could be written about. She had put her life on the line many times, and that was why she had become so successful.

The story she had just finished would be her best yet. Perhaps ever.

And that opinion was echoed by her editor, Joe Bannon, a rotund man who looked sixty, was closer to fifty and revered the written word. "You know you've done a brilliant job. You also know you look like hell, and need more time to recuperate than you're asking for. Two weeks is not enough!" he had exclaimed. "More than a month wouldn't be enough for you in the shape you're in!" He tried to bend his roly-poly body over the desk as he hunched toward her.

She was slumped in a straight-backed chair, hardly able to keep her head up. She had returned three days earlier from her ordeal in Central America and, after a brief hospital stay, had gone straight to a hotel room, pounding away at a rented typewriter with a blurred *e*, writing copy for the photos she had processed earlier.

Who would have believed her captors would have returned her luggage and the exposed film? They had even allowed her to take a farewell picture of them as a memento! The piece was good, sharp, concise. Her best. And her boss knew it. But right now she didn't give a damn about the story or anything else.

"Two weeks, Joe. Then I'll phone in to see what else is on the schedule," she insisted, combating the floating feeling that suddenly seemed to take charge of her head and limbs. Her torso was leaden, but the rest of her wanted to soar.

"Hope, I don't think you realize what bad shape you're in. You're exhausted. You've been starved and threatened. Don't you have sense enough to call it quits for a while?"

His words drifted in and out of her small sphere of reality. He kept on ranting, but as she watched him with mild curiosity, he disappeared in a cloud of bright white light that pierced her eyes. She moaned once, squeezing them shut before the floor rushed up to meet her.

Within the hour she was back in the hospital—this time in Chicago. Five days later she was released with dire warnings about recovering her health before going back to work. An hour after her discharge she was packed and on her way to the airport. She was delivered to a flight bound for Duluth, where a car waited to take her into the Arrowhead area of northeast Minnesota, just beyond Two Harbors. Punctuated by flashing blue lakes, dotted by dollops of fern-green islands and dense with surrounding forest, it was one of the most beautiful spots in the world. Once there, she took a small motorboat to her island, situated just below Superior National Forest on the edge of the Boundary Waters Canoe Area.

She was unable to control the direction of her thoughts. Her mind skipped back over the past year, refreshing and enlightening her with the wisdom of clear hindsight. Her boss had always employed her talents to the fullest, making sure she got two- and three-week assignments with good potential. She'd been sent to France, then come back home only to fly out to Egypt, then home again, then South America.

Despite the rigors of such a hectic schedule, she had jumped at the assignment in Central America because her father was living there at the time. It was a chance to renew a relationship that had never had the cement of familiarity to begin with. After her parents' divorce when she was twelve, Hope had moved to Minneapolis, where her mother began a career in computer programming. With the exception of short, awkward visits, Hope and her father never saw or corresponded with each other. The breach had widened until, when Hope was seventeen and her mother died, her father hadn't even attended the funeral. From that time on, Hope had referred to her father by his given name, Frank. It was easier to keep distance that way.

But time had a way of healing wounds, and she had been ready to make peace when the Central American assignment came up. Only she hadn't been there twenty-four hours when a suburban uprising had evolved into a full-scale, heavily armed, first-class civil war.

Hope and her father's secretary, Joanne, were kidnapped, taken at gunpoint from a car returning them to Frank's hacienda from a shopping spree in the city. For the first two weeks they were held in a dark, musty cellar somewhere in the city. Then, because the U.S. government couldn't make up its mind whether or not to pay the ransom, and because her publisher couldn't, the kidnapping became enmeshed in negotiation.

Hope and Joanne were separated. Hope was held captive in the jungle, the cruelest jail of all, for two months, barely making do with insufficient food and no sanitary facilities. It wasn't until after her release that she realized just how lucky she had been. Joanne hadn't made it back at all....

But now she was out and safe, cared for by friends like her editor, Joe. Joe had taken care of everything, including stocking enough food to last a few weeks. When that ran out, she could head back to the mainland and replenish her supplies. He had been wonderful as a boss... and a friend, worthy of the name.

Hope glanced at the roll of film in her hand. She'd develop it tomorrow. Any tomorrow. Time no longer mattered. Setting it on her darkroom counter, she flipped off the light and went on down the hall to her bedroom, heading toward the window as she began to unbutton her blouse. She slipped out of her jeans, leaving them in a small faded puddle on the floor. There was no bra to join the pile. There were no underpants tonight, either. That choice had felt distinctly odd and, strangely enough, defiant. She didn't have to wear anything if she didn't want to. Not here.

Naked, she stood in front of the second-story window and stared out at the small knoll that rose from the back and side of her "yard." Moonlight flowed over her skin, making it translucent, as if she were glowing from the inside. Wherever the moon touched her, she felt a warmth, a caressing, as if a gentle hand was stroking her flesh.

Hope shivered. She must need the company of a man desperately to have such strong, if fleeting, thoughts of making love while staring at a hillside! Her mind was playing tricks on her again, as it had in the jungle prison. As it had that afternoon when she was sitting by the rock at the top of the hill. Perhaps she was lonelier than she had thought. Had Joe been correct when he had declared she needed more than a month's rest? Maybe thinking about making love was a way to wipe out bad memories. . . .

The following day was beautiful, a tourist ad for the ideal Minnesota summer vacation. The sun sparkled on the water. The gaily colored sails of a small sloop could be seen bobbing in a cove about a mile away. Even the air was tepid, a breeze blowing barely enough to flutter the fine lace curtains that gracefully framed the windows.

She had slept through the night in a sleep deeper than any she had experienced in months. Energy filled her to the brim, causing a tingle to shimmy all the way down to her fingertips. Today was not a day to lie around.

Within half an hour, breakfast had been eaten and the kitchen cleaned, and she was ready to develop her film.

Mixing the developing chemicals was second nature to her, and she did it with a minimum of fuss. The film was developed quickly in a portable tank. Now came the best part: turning the negatives into prints.

Ever since she could remember, Hope had loved photography. For her, the real creativity came in when the negatives became photographs; shadow and light could be toyed with, the definition of the lines softened or accented. This time in the darkroom often made the difference between an ordinary photo and a great one. This was the fun time.

For a moment she thought of making a contact sheet of the photos, to see which ones she wanted to blow up. Then she discarded the idea in favor of printing each picture separately. This was her vacation, not actual work where she had to decide what would produce the most money in the shortest amount of time. She grinned. A busman's holiday.

One by one, she framed each negative in the enlarger and focused the image on the paper, switching the bright light on and off at the sound of the timer. Then she swished the exposed paper around in the chemical tanks and watched the images come to life before hanging the sheets to dry on a small clothesline above the counter. She worked efficiently in the rosy glow cast by the lamp she had fitted with a red bulb, long habit controlling her movements. Soon all the prints were in the solution trays, or being washed or dried.

She hummed a soft, wordless melody, stopping only when she realized she'd never heard the tune before. Without thinking, she had started humming it yesterday while up at the rock.

Shrugging her shoulders as if to rid herself of introspective ramblings, she checked the rinse tray, then did a double take.

Something was wrong. Very wrong.

Bending over, she peered into the water at the black-and-white print floating there. It was supposed to be a picture she had snapped of the rock yesterday. The rock was there, smaller than she remembered it, but so were small white flames darting across the paper.

She continued to stare long after she had absorbed every detail. Once again, the small hairs on the back of her neck bristled, just as they had yesterday. Making certain the unexposed paper was in the closed cabinet, she pulled the cord that filled the tiny room with light.

"I must be insane!" she muttered as she lifted the dripping photo from the water and stared at it as if her eyes could wipe out the small silver-white darts. "Now I'm imagining ghosts when all this is is damaged paper." Water dripped from her trembling hand and stained the polished oak floor a darker hue. There had to be a reason. There should be something or someone to blame for this, this... "Someone was sloppy when they unpacked my equipment. That's all," she reassured herself.

Hope looked down at the print again, then at a few others, hardly daring to check the rest, yet knowing even before she did that only the pictures of the large rock on the top of the bluff would have the flawed paper. Her heartbeat quickened. She was right.

Once again she went over the photos. The small streaks resembled the figures of men standing in a rough semicircle. No features were visible, but legs and arms shot out from the streaks as if the figures were imprisoned by lightning.

Impossible. Her stomach clutched at what her mind refused to accept.

She turned out the overhead light and began again. Reaching into the cabinet under the enlarger, she pulled out a larger sheet of paper and began the process of blowing up a small portion of the rock, where the darts of silver seemed to etch the stone itself. She timed the exposure, then slipped the paper directly into the developing solution, tapping her foot impatiently until the first faint images began to appear.

Eyes widening, she sucked in her breath. Those little darts of white weren't darts at all. With shaking hands, she picked up her tongs and swished the photo back and forth, then moved it into the tray of fixing solution before washing it and hanging it on the makeshift clothesline above her head. There were five photos of the large rock, all with the darts of light. Now she would blow up the other four. Forcing herself to move slowly, methodically, she set to work. If her suspicions were correct, she'd be all day puzzling out this mystery.

LATE AFTERNOON found Hope leaning against her bedroom window, staring out at the top of the small bluff. Funny. She had been visiting this island all her life, and she'd owned it for the past nine years. At one time or another, she had traversed the length and breadth of her small kingdom, exploring this, examining that. For the second time in two days, she recalled having felt that someone or something was always watching her. Or watching over her. When she grew older, Hope had shoved away those feelings, telling herself it was only a lonely child's overactive imagination.

But now it was time for the adult in her to face up to the past, to delve into that feeling—that eerie yet comforting feeling. Those pictures, now dry, had to be evaluated. All five had been enlarged, and each one confirmed her original impression. There were men up there. And they weren't real men, not today's men. Spirits? Ghosts?

She had to take more pictures. She had to find out more about those men and the strange rock.

She reached for her camera, loaded it and almost ran out the back door toward the top of the hill. There had to be answers!

When she came within fifty feet of the rock, she felt a presence. What kind, and whether it was good or bad, she couldn't tell. But this time, perhaps she'd find proof that she wasn't crazy....

She clicked the shutter, shooting from one angle, then quickly from another, and another and another. She knelt, bent, sat and stood, approaching from every possible angle to photograph the large boulder.

When her film was exhausted, she sat down on the ground. Her mind whirled with possibilities. None of them overrode the feeling of being watched. She leaned against the rock, relishing its warmth and the fresh dampness of the breeze, which carried the threat of a storm. Usually, no matter what season, the evenings were cool to downright cold. But not tonight. Not at the rock, at least. How strange.

Before it grew too dark for her to see her way clearly, she decided to take the path down the hill. Levering her shoulders away from the stone, she had the eeriest sensation that someone was actually holding her, imprisoning her with a comforting warmth that reached around her like loving arms. Despite the nonthreatening feeling, panic rose in her throat, and she shoved herself against the force, standing up and propelling herself toward the path.

As soon as she escaped, logic returned.

This was impossible. She turned and stared back at the rock once more as night slowly swept down over the island. The thing was just a rock with moonlight glinting off the silver particles of mica embedded in it. Nothing more.

Just a rock.

Dark clouds scudded across the brilliant full moon, boiling with their impatience to release the weight of their water. Rain would come in torrents tonight, she was sure.

Deliberately pushing away the thoughts of ghosts on her island, she entered the house and made her way upstairs to bed and drifted into a deep sleep.

Morning turned out to be as wet as she had silently predicted. Even so, she felt better, more rested than ever. After a quick breakfast Hope was in the darkroom, developing what she had thought so important yesterday, but which would doubtless look silly in the morning light.

Two hours later, the film developed, her pounding heart thudded in her ears. She sat at the kitchen table, the pictures fanned out across the surface. She had played with their order until, like the pieces of a jigsaw puzzle, she thought she had them in the right sequence.

She saw four men fighting in a clearing, three of them dressed like voyageurs. The French trappers had come to this area hundreds of years ago seeking the animal pelts that had clothed the European aristocracy. In the last photo, one of the men lay mortally wounded. He was the one wearing an old-fashioned military uniform, an elegant coat reaching down to his knees and a tricorne hat at his side.

She stared at the picture, trying to make out his facial features, but they were just hazy enough to be muted. Some event up there by the rock was being reenacted again and again. How old were these men, and what were they doing on her island? She really should be more frightened than she was. Ghosts, in any form, should scare her.

She picked up one of the pictures and studied it closely. Through a magnifying glass, she stared at each part of the uniform, straining to recall information stored long ago. She didn't know why she thought so, but she was almost sure the uniform was French.

Then her mind began clicking like a ticker-tape machine. French. Of course! This territory, along with parts of Michigan and Canada, had been fought over by the French and the British, with the voyageur trappers sometimes caught in the middle.

But what year was that? Mentally she dredged up past history classes, churning over facts she thought were long forgotten. Champlain had been the first to discover the value of the fine furs of what was now Canada. But word spread swiftly, and soon there were hundreds of Frenchmen settling in what was dubbed "New France," making their fortunes in shipping furs to the Europeans. Then the British came to Canada's Hudson Bay, and the French and Indian War followed. That was sometime in the mid-1700s, she was almost certain.

"My God," she whispered, realizing suddenly that this wasn't a figment of her imagination. These photographs were real; the situation depicted was real. Excitement blossomed in the pit of her stomach. It ran the length of her body, tingling down to the tips of the fingers holding the photo, and to the tips of her toes.

Lightning cracked, and thunder erupted right behind it. Large raindrops rat-tat-tatted against the kitchen window, hammering for her attention.

Her mind totally absorbed with the photos, Hope didn't notice nature's floor show. She glanced at the scenery in the photographs again, her eye catching on a small sapling near the men. A sapling? She remembered it as a huge oak! Could that be the same tree?

She jumped from the chair, a photo still in hand, and dashed for the back door. With a leap worthy of an Olympic sprinter, she was off the back porch and headed toward the path to the top of the hill. Rain poured from the clouds, but she didn't feel it. Dodging trees and branches, she was aware of her feet sliding in the mud and moss amid the rivulets flowing down the hillside. By the time she was halfway to the top, her warm-up suit was soaked through. It hung like a lead weight from her shoulders and waist. With quick, fluid movements she shed it, then kicked off her running shoes.

She ran the rest of the way, hair streaming behind her in thick strands of dark, shining satin. When she reached the top, she halted, gasping. She realized she had no breath left to climb the twenty or so feet to the base of the boulder.

Lightning raked the sky again. As it did, she held the photo in front of her, wiping raindrops from her eyes as she peered at the huge, dripping oak tree positioned against the boulder. Excitement mounted in her like a tidal wave. Damn! She was right; it was the same tree! And the same eggplant-shaped boulder!

She laughed aloud into the wind, her arms in the air as she yelled her excitement. "Eureka!" she screamed to the sky. And the sky answered with a thunderbolt that reached out to stab the boulder, the mind-shattering sound immediately echoing its anger.

The last thing she remembered was the rock glowing brilliantly; then her hair stiffened as she was thrown to the earth by the electrical power of the thunderbolt. Her head hit a gnarled tree root that time and the elements had exposed. Then everything was dark.

2

A CALLUSED HAND gently stroked her brow. A rough, deep voice muttered a curse or a prayer; Hope wasn't sure which. Goose bumps played along her bare legs. Fat raindrops dripped from the oak towering above her. Oddly, her torso and arms were warm. She snuggled into that warmth, her eyes closed tight. A throbbing on the side of her head prevented her from sinking back into a blissful nothingness.

"Faith! Oh, my Faith, please wake up, *chérie!*" the deep voice implored her, and her eyelids fluttered open to see who was disturbing her rest. Her head throbbed like a drum.

She moved her lips, but no sound came out. She tried again. This time, his mouth closed over hers, and he let a sigh of relief escape. His mouth was warm, even warmer than the arms holding her. His touch was so soft, so gentle, so sweet . . .

She jerked her head away, some remote part of her brain screaming that she didn't even know who was holding her, attempting to kiss her back into the world. She tried to focus her eyes, but no matter how hard she tried, she saw two of him.

Two dark heads were bent over her. Brows furrowed above indigo-blue eyes revealed concern. Two shocks of ebony hair fell almost to his shoulders. Two mouths were speaking sweetly hushed endearments, and two hands stroked back her wet hair. He touched the bump on her head and she winced.

"Ouch," she complained, her hand trapping his thick wrist so that he couldn't hurt her again.

"Oh, darling," he crooned. "I am so sorry, my Faith. Does it hurt very much?"

"Like hell," she said with a grunt. She tried unsuccessfully to push herself up. But his arms were too strong, and his grip too sure. "Who the hell is Faith?"

"Do not curse," he ordered. "You always did have a difficulty keeping your mouth closed at the right time." He sounded gruff, but the smile that dimpled his handsome face gave him away as relief flooded his eyes. She studied the beautifully mobile lips, so fascinated that she was no longer aware of the chilling air.

"Faith?" His dark brows drew together again. "My darling, are you feeling better? Do you remember what happened?" His fingers lingered a moment on her bare waist, then traveled up to cup her breast in his warm hand. "What are you doing here, so far away from Port Huron?" His questions were rapid-fire. "And why did you come to me with no clothing? Surely, you were not so eager . . . ?"

He might not have thought she was eager, but his hopes had certainly been high, Hope thought as she moved her shoulder against his powerful thigh and felt the stirrings of basic desire. Her mind was a jumble of confusion, her emotions working by instinct. Finally she struggled from his tender grasp and sat up across from him on the spongy moss under the broad spreading oak branches.

He had to be tall, because even with his knees on the ground, he towered above her. "Who are you?" she asked, pushing aside her hair and staring up at him.

She ignored her own nudity, because there was nothing she could do about it. Besides, her logical mind told her he should be the one who was embarrassed. After all, it was her island, not his!

"Do you not remember?" His voice was soft but raspy, like rough velvet, with just a hint of an accent. French, that was it. He was French. She glanced at his shoulders, measuring him. And his uniform was French. It was the same as the man in the photos.

The man in the pictures! Her eyes darted to his again. Now that she could see his face, she wondered how she could have missed the resemblance before. He was as familiar and handsome to her as the fantasy lover of her own dreams.

"You're the man in the picture!" she whispered. Another blistering crack of lightning punctuated her sentence.

He frowned. "You have a portrait of me? But you never told me that before, *chérie*. When was it done? By whom?" As he spoke he shrugged out of his uniform jacket, revealing a beautifully cut white shirt fitted snugly across his chest, with full sleeves buttoned at his wrists. The shoulder padding of the jacket was minimal; his shoulders were just as broad without the extra fabric. He tucked the jacket around her and she hugged it to her, more aware of the chilling dampness now that his body heat was gone.

Without thinking, she shook her head and became even dizzier than before. She stopped immediately, placing a hand to her head as if to stop the motion. "No, no, no. Not a painting, a picture. You know, a photograph."

His frown deepened. Then he smiled, and she felt his warmth come flooding back. "You have a big bump on your head, darling. You will feel better in a little while," he said, as if that explained everything. "Meanwhile, come back into my arms and let me keep you warm until this squall ends. Although the branches are shielding us from most of the rain, it must be chilling you. Then we must leave immediately."

Leave? Immediately? *Now* who was crazy? She smiled, even as a shiver swept over her body. It was best to humor him. After all, it surely wasn't every day he saw a naked woman sitting under a tree in a thunderstorm. And it was no less unusual for her to find a man in a uniform who looked as if he came out of a museum, either! Somewhere in the back of her mind she knew she should be asking him questions before he disappeared. Logically, she knew that she was talking to a ghost, but emotionally she couldn't seem to get her act together. "And where are we going that we have to leave so quickly?"

A dark, arrogant brow lifted above a clear blue eye. "To France, of course."

"Of course," she muttered, pushing a dripping strand of hair behind her ear. Then she remembered more. If he was here, where were the other three men from the photos? Her gaze darted to the shadowed bushes and trees, trying to locate other outlines. It was one thing to meet a ghost, but it was another to meet four of them! And the other three had looked dangerous. Suddenly she laughed. As if those months in Central America hadn't been enough to send her off the deep end, now she could claim to be frightened of four ghosts!

But he couldn't be a ghost! He was so solid. All over! Could ghosts have erections?

She stopped laughing and stared at him. He moved toward her, and she edged backward until the tree trunk behind her blocked her way. Breath caught in her throat as she looked into his eyes. When she raised a hand in protest, her other hand held the lapels of his jacket together. "You stay back. Just stay there until we get this mess straightened out."

His arms were outstretched, imploring her. "Faith, my darling, what is the matter? Do you not know I would not harm you for the world!" He looked so lost, so loving. Except Hope had seen the glint in his eyes as he begged so sweetly. He wanted to do more than protect her. . . .

"Just hold it there a damn minute, buster," she said threateningly, her eyes blazing at him, her posture telling him better than her words exactly how she felt about being wrapped in his arms. She raised a finger of her free hand. "First. My name is Hope, not Faith." Another finger went up. "Second. You're a ghost. I might be stupid enough to sit here and discuss running away with you in a rainstorm, but I'm sure not stupid enough to fall into your loving arms!"

If she could have captured the look on his face with her camera, the film would have portrayed complete and utter shock. She wanted to laugh, to shout, to scream. On the other hand, she couldn't control the shivering that had begun around the vicinity of her spine and echoed throughout her entire body. It wasn't from the cold; it was from nerves.

He cleared his throat, then gave her a wan smile, but Hope knew something she had said had registered in his mind. He looked down and flexed his fingers, long fingers that looked capable of playing a difficult sonata on a piano. "But surely I am not a ghost, *chérie*. I am here. You are here. Do these look like the hands of a spirit?"

"No, but that's what you are, just the same." She stared at him, wondering once more if she was crazy and he was sane. Even to herself she sounded irrational, but then the whole situation, beginning with the photos, had been irrational! "Either you're a ghost or a refugee from an asylum." She took a deep breath, then offered him a shaky smile. Perhaps if she ignored the thumping in her head and had time to gather her thoughts together, her mind would start working better. "I know," she said. "Why don't you tell me about yourself, and then I'll tell you about me?"

His deep blue eyes opened wide, a frown marring his high, strong brow. Then he shrugged his shoulders under that fine lawn shirt and smiled, as if to humor her. "I am Armand Santeuil."

"Santoy?"

He nodded.

"How do you spell that?"

"Just the way it sounds. S-a-n-t-e-u-i-l. I am a captain in the French army, sent here—never mind why, you will remember later—and you and I fell in love. Remember?" He waited for her reaction, but there was none other than her fixed smile. He continued. "I finally persuaded you to leave your father's care and meet me outside Port Huron. Then we were leaving for France immediately, where we would marry and continue a line of little Santeuils." His smile lit up the area under the tree with a dazzling light. "You promised me at least ten of them."

Hope's mouth dropped open. "Ten children?"

"*Oui.*"

"Faith must have been built like a Sherman tank," she muttered.

Once more he frowned. "What is this Sherman tank?"

She waved a vague hand in the air. "Never mind. Continue."

She could sense his irritation at her imperious command, but her mind was too busy to cope with his confusion. It was probably nothing compared to her own, anyway. Any minute she was sure she'd find herself under this tree, soaking wet and shivering with cold, awakening from a dream.

"Continue with what? That is it," he stated. "Now it is your turn to remember." His hand reached out to stroke a strand of wet hair off her cheek. His touch was warm, his hand substantial yet sensuous against her skin. Without realizing it, she leaned toward him, almost craving his touch. Quickly she backed away.

A ghost! He was a ghost! She kept repeating that fact to herself. And she still didn't really know a thing about him. Not even if he was the good guy or the bad. If he was good, why did the other three men kill him? Surely he must have done something wrong for them to attack him.

Her mind spun again, and to slow it down and buy more time to think, she began talking. "My name is Hope Langston. I work as a photojournalist for one of the top magazines in the country. I travel all over, then return here to work and rest. This is my island, it's been in my family for quite a few years."

He shook his head slowly, a faint but sympathetic smile playing about his sensuous lips. "Tsk, tsk, tsk. No, *chérie*. Do not attempt to deceive me. You are Faith Trevor. Your father is a British officer recently sent to Port Huron in the New France territory that is attached to the colonies. He refused us his permission to marry, and we decided to do so against his wishes." He smiled. "You are my betrothed." His blue eyes seared right through her. "Do you remember now, *chérie*?"

"No," she snapped. "I hate to burst your bubble, buster, but I'm not your '*chérie*.' I am who I say I am, and this is almost the 1990s. The state is called Minnesota and is part of the United States of America. You are dead, and I am not." She hesitated. The confusion on his face was obvious. He thought she had gone mad. "In your time, whenever it was, no woman would take off all her clothes and run about in the rain. In my time, it is possible."

He put a hand to his brow. "*Mon Dieu, chérie*. We are not in the future. This is the year 1762. Has that bump affected your memory? Perhaps it is worse than I first believed." Once more he tried to gather her into his arms, but she resisted again.

"No!" she shouted. "You don't understand! I'm the one who belongs here, not you! This is *my* time, not yours!" He continued to hold on to her arms, dragging her inexorably against his broad chest. Frantically she glanced around, searching for a weapon, any weapon she could use against him. Suddenly she stopped struggling and he stopped pulling, watching her carefully, warily. Her thoughts buzzed. What weapons do you use against a ghost? Her cross?

As if in slow motion, her hand rose to locate the chain at her neck. It was still there, the gold cross suspended from it. Armand followed her hand with his eyes, his sturdy grip loosening a bit to permit her slow movement. Their eyes locked, brown eyes staring into blue.

Then she remembered. Crosses were useful only against vampires, not ghosts. Her mind began whirling once more. "I'll prove it to you," she whispered.

"How?"

"Let me get my running suit."

"Running suit? What is this . . . running suit?"

"That's the clothing I was wearing when I was coming up the hill. It was soaking wet and heavy, so I took it off, but it shouldn't be more than thirty feet from here."

He hesitated for a fraction of a second, then apparently decided to humor her. "I will go with you."

Another lightning bolt crackled across the sky as he stood up. The rain suddenly turned to a light, misty drizzle. He reached down and clasped her hands to help her stand. For the tiniest moment she was desperate to pry her hands from his; his grip was too sure, too frightening. He was also much too male, and that reminded her of the days and nights in Central America. Intense fear, and a bad bump on the head, had made her queasy. The mixture was far too volatile for her to cope with readily. But before she could protest, he released her hands and was at her side, a deepening frown silently questioning her next move.

She wrapped his coat more tightly around her and walked along the path that led down the hill. After sloping downward, the path leveled off for about ten feet, creating a small plateau. Her running-suit top was lying there in the mud, its brilliant blue turned to a rusty brown from soil and rain.

She picked it up, wringing it out as best she could, stalling for time. But when she turned to go back up the hill, she found him right behind her.

He stood quietly, hands braced on his hips, one leg splayed out as he adjusted his balance on the slanting hill. He looked so rugged. His wet shirt clung, outlining every muscle. His dark gold pants were nearly as tight as a woman's hose, and they disappeared into the shiny black calf-hugging Hessian boots just below his knees. Without his elegant gold braided jacket he looked more like a pirate than an officer of the French army. He was also looking very angry and a touch confused.

"All right, my Faith. What is it about this filthy lump of material that will prove your delusions are correct?"

"This." She held out the front of the jacket.

He bent his head, staring intently. His long, elegant fingers probed the fabric, rubbing the damp velour sensually.

Hope shook the material. "Not the fabric, the zipper."

"The what?"

He was humoring her again, even though they both knew he wasn't understanding half the words she used.

"The zipper," she explained patiently. "The fastening that closes this garment was invented in the early twentieth century and is used on almost all clothing now." She gathered the bottom edges of the jacket and fastened them together, then lifted the tab and pulled. "See?"

He took the garment from her hands, studying it closely before trying the zipper himself. Without looking at her, he tried it several times, muttering under his breath. He spoke absently, as if she were there only to answer his questions. "Did the French invent this?"

"Good grief," she groaned. "I don't know, and that's not important! The point is that it was invented after you were gone!"

As if insulted, he stiffened, his blue eyes focusing on her. "The French have long been the leaders of fashion. We are very proud of that, and so should you be, my Faith, if you are to become French."

She smiled sweetly, although her eyes shot sparks of gold fire at him. "I'm not going to be. And my name is Hope."

For the first time, she could see that he was beginning to doubt his own convictions. Not that everything she had said made sense to him, but at least some of it seemed to be getting through. Suddenly she remembered her original reason for coming up the hill.

"Oh! Come here!" she exclaimed, forgetting to hold the uniform coat together as she grabbed his hand and began running up the hill, dragging him behind her. "I'll show you!"

There it was. The photograph she had dropped in the moss at the base of the rock was soggy and muddy, but it could still be used to prove the difference between his time and hers. "See? This is what I came up here for! I took this yesterday along with some others. It's of you!" Her hands shook as she wiped them on his jacket and handed him the photo.

His dark blue eyes clouded as he studied the photo. Cautiously he looked at the back of the flimsy paper, then at the front again. Suddenly he froze, his gaze seeking out the smoky figures that she had first seen. When he spoke, his voice was rough with emotion. "What is this called?"

"A photograph."

"And how do you make it?"

"I aim my camera and click open the lens. The camera holds the image of whatever I shoot on something called film, which absorbs the light and leaves an image." She explained the process, even though she knew he didn't really understand.

"How long does that take?"

She realized he couldn't possibly absorb all that she was saying. How could he when he didn't even know what a camera was? "About a second or two to take the picture, then another hour to develop it."

His eyes narrowed, burning her with blue flame. "Are you making a fool of me? Is this a joke?"

Slowly she shook her head. She could understand his reluctance to believe. Wouldn't she feel the same way if she were in his shoes? "No. This is what I do for a living."

"Mon Dieu," he whispered. He leaned against the rock and stared at the evidence in his hands. "This is not seventeen and sixty-two."

"No." Her voice was a hoarse whisper. Her toes curled into the wet moss.

He looked at her, his eyes filled with despair. "And even though you are her image, you are not my Faith."

"No," she whispered, somehow wishing that she were, wishing she could erase the awful hurt in his eyes.

"And yet I am alive."

Hope didn't answer. She didn't know what to say.

But he persisted. "Feel me! Feel my heart! Am I alive to you? Do I not breath the air you breathe, touch the things you touch?" He grabbed her hand and thrust it to his chest. His heartbeat was strong and sturdy.

Thunder rumbled in the distance. The storm was abating, leaving behind a dreary, overcast day. Even the drizzle had stopped.

"I see you. I feel you. But I don't know if you're alive or not." Her eyes pleaded for him to understand her confusion, but he was too immersed in his own misery to help her. She sighed, tucking a strand of wet hair behind her ear. "Come back to the house with me. We'll talk this over while I get warm."

He stared at the photograph in his hand, then nodded his head. "*Oui*, we will do that."

Her bare feet dragged through the soaked moss and wet leaves as she led the way toward the path. She knew he was following behind her because she could feel his presence, just as she had as a child, and as she had lately. It was a strong, gentle presence that seemed to care for her.

They edged carefully down the hill, Hope leading their parade of two toward the bottom of the hill, and the house. Just before she reached level ground, she heard his curse and spun around to see him standing stock-still, hands held in front of him, palms toward her.

"What's the matter?" She walked back two steps until she was within touching distance of him.

"I cannot go farther." His voice was dark with surprise and frustration. He moved his palms in the air as if he was banging against something. His actions reminded Hope of a mime she had once seen in New York. He had pretended there was a wall of glass between him and the audience. Only Armand was no mime. . . .

Reaching out tentatively, she touched the front of his shirt. The barrier disappeared. "Come, hold my hand."

He tried, but couldn't reach it until he had stepped back a pace.

"Now try," she coaxed, trying to remain calm even though her mind was whirling. What in hell was happening?

He stepped forward, only to be stopped again. His dark blue eyes shot sparks of frustration, and Hope swore there were tears filming his eyes. Then he closed them and lifted his face to the heavens, breathing deeply. When he opened them again, he was staring at her, his eyes once more revealing total desolation. "I am dead." It was no longer a question. It was the answer.

"Try again."

He shook his head, his eyes never leaving hers. "It will not work. I am dead, and am nothing more than a haunting. I must stay here. I know that now."

"No!" she cried, tugging on his hand. She wanted him with her in the house. She wanted him by her side. But it was no use. The invisible wall was still there, and he was caught on the other side.

Tears of frustration ran down her cheeks, mingling with the dampness on her skin. She bowed her head, not even trying to hide her own emotions.

He pulled her hand as he took several steps backward, drawing her into the warm comfort of his arms. "Never mind, *chérie*, I should have known. Even the countryside looks different, now that I study it carefully." He pressed the side of her face against his shirt, and she could hear the steady pounding of his heart. "Truly, I think I did know this thing, but I did not want to admit it."

She sniffled. "Why?"

"Because I thought you were my Faith, and God was sweet and merciful enough to return you to me."

"What happens now?" She leaned away, embarrassed at her lack of restraint. If she was decadent enough to run around naked, she should be worldly-wise enough to handle meeting a gentlemanly ghost!

He gave a small sad smile and a very Gallic shrug. "Who knows, *chérie*? Perhaps I will be here like this for all of eternity. Mayhap I will disappear again tonight and yet find my Faith waiting for me."

"But why are you here? There must be a reason. There's always a reason!"

"Oh? And how many ghosts have you known?" He smoothed back her hair, cradling her face gently in his large, strong hands.

"None," she finally admitted.

"Not even one or two?"

She couldn't help the smile that dimpled her cheeks. "No."

He responded by allowing the twinkle in his blue eyes to warm her. "Then I am the first?"

"Yes," she said, chuckling. This was so damn funny, it was ludicrous! Here she was, stark naked under an old French army jacket, and talking to a ghost!

"*Alors.* We are even. You are the first person I have spoken to since I have been a ghost."

Her brows shot up. "How do you know?" she asked. "I mean, if you didn't realize you were a ghost until a few minutes ago, how could you know to whom you've talked over the centuries?"

Amusement still sparkled in his eyes. "I just know. That is all. I would have remembered, just as I am beginning to remember other things." He stared over her shoulder across the water toward the distant shoreline.

"Like what?"

"Like I did not know for sure whether or not my Faith would defy her father and come to me. I was certain of my love, but I was not sure of hers."

He must feel such pain from waiting and not knowing if his patience had been in vain, Hope thought. So many questions popped into her head, questions to which there were no answers. But somehow she would get answers, she was sure. "Armand, stay on the hill. I'm going to clean up and get dressed. Then I'll fix a meal and bring it out to eat with you."

His eyes focused on hers once more, bringing them both back to the present, and she felt a velvet arrow of warmth plummet toward her stomach. "Good," he said. "Because I am starved!"

"I don't know, but I'm sure all the etiquette books state that ghosts aren't supposed to get hungry."

"Well, this one is," he said with certainty.

She grinned cheekily as she turned and strolled, with increasing purposefulness, the rest of the way to the house.

3

HER SMILE FADED QUICKLY to a frown when Hope closed the door behind her. Closing her eyes, she leaned against the cool wood and listened to the silence of the house. Okay, she was crazy. Central America had driven her over the brink, and Armand's presence was a delayed reaction to the mental strain. She had become too relaxed, too casual about her recovery, and her mind was beginning to play devious little tricks on her.

Her eyes popped open. No. He had been real. As real as she was. She tiptoed to the window over the sink and stared out toward the base of the hill. He was gone.

She'd been right the first time. She *was* crazy. Her heart beat in double time. Now she was frightened of herself.

Had that whole scene—Armand, the thunderstorm, his inability to leave the hill—had it all been imaginary? Had she wanted so badly to believe that there were good men to contrast with the beasts who had been her captors these past months? Could it have been her mind's way of finding some semblance of sanity in this insane world?

Hope slumped into a wooden chair at the kitchen table. Resting her head on her arms, she closed her eyes. She rubbed her cheek against the coarse fabric of Armand's coat and smelled rain, damp earth and his own indefinable scent.

Suddenly her head shot up. She had his jacket! Maybe he was a ghost, but she hadn't dreamed him up! She slipped the coat off and studied it more carefully. Even as she was staring at it, it began to age, tiny threads dissolving and tattering, its color fading from bright gold to a dingy peach brown. Once-shiny silver-and-gold braiding on the shoulders and sleeves tarnished to a dirty gray. She smoothed her hand along a sleeve as it transformed slowly to a shabby rag before her eyes. Tears filmed her vision, and she lifted the jacket to her nose again. His scent was still there. Through the tears came her smile.

Clutching the jacket to her breast, she ran upstairs. She turned on the bathtub taps, then grabbed a pair of jeans and a dark brown sweater from her bedroom.

Carefully placing the jacket on the small counter next to the sink so she could keep an eye on it, she stepped into the steaming bath.

As she sank into the water, it dawned on her that she felt warm for the first time since she had pulled away from the soldier's—Armand's—strong arms. That thought sent a shiver down her spine. She sunk lower into the water, tipped her head back and washed her hair.

Okay, big girl. Now what?

Faith. A young woman who couldn't choose between her father and her lover. Apparently she hadn't had the courage to buck her father to be with the man she loved. Hadn't she realized that what her soldier felt for her was more than most women ever glimpsed in an entire lifetime?

Hope shook her head. Here she was, getting all wrapped up in a romantic love story when it had no bearing on her. In fact his damn story was more than two hundred years old!

She shivered again and climbed out of the tub, wrapping a large blue bath sheet around herself. It took her less than five minutes to dress, but it was twenty minutes before her thick mane of hair was dry. Then another ten minutes to find something she could put together that resembled a picnic. Her menu included a $3.99 California Chablis, four peanut-butter-and-honey sandwiches on whole wheat, and some carrot and celery sticks, along with a plastic tub of onion dip.

Grinning, she looked over the items spread out on the wooden kitchen table. She hoped he wasn't a French-food gourmet; if he was, she was in serious trouble. Creams and sauces were definitely not her thing. Besides, they were fattening.

What was she thinking of? Since Central America, her jeans hung loose on her hips. Perhaps she should attempt to eat some fattening foods. Heaven knew, she could use the extra weight.

Throwing her goodies into a grocery bag along with some plastic glasses, she searched around for a tablecloth. Then she remembered and raced upstairs, not bothering to catch her breath as she ran to the old trunk in the spare bedroom. Dragging the stuff out to litter the floor, she finally found what she was looking for: a plastic-lined sheet her mother had bought and never used. It was clean, scented by the wild lilies of the valley her mother used to pick and dry. Perfect.

In another five minutes she was packed and out the door, walking briskly toward the path to the top of the hill.

Would he still be there, or had he disappeared as quickly as he had come? Questions multiplied and grew. For every answer, another million questions sprouted in her mind.

She climbed the hill slowly, beginning to believe that she would be picnicking by herself. He would be gone, and she'd be alone on the hill, just as she had been before.

Probably the only reason that she had felt him so strongly before was that he had been so certain she was his Faith; he had been reaching out to her. Now that he knew better, he'd most likely head for wherever old ghosts were supposed to go.

All the way up the hill she prepared herself for his absence. When she reached the top and stepped under the large oak tree, she realized she had been right.

No one was there.

An indescribable disappointment flooded over her. Carefully, deliberately, she unfolded the plastic sheet and spread it just so on the ground. Sitting cross-legged with the cloth under her, she unscrewed the metal cap of the wine bottle, poured some wine into a plastic glass and gulped down a large swallow. She was going to have fun on her first picnic in years if it killed her—with or without a certain mysterious French officer's company!

As if she were setting up a shot, she placed the food on the cloth. That done, she took another swallow of wine. At this rate she wouldn't care whether he was here or not . . . she'd be too drunk to notice!

A lightly whistled tune caught her attention. A melody, faintly familiar to her, drifted on the late-morning air currents. She raised her head, her wide brown eyes darting to a far clump of trees, her slight frame poised for flight. That tune. That haunting melody was the one she had been humming earlier. She knew that she had never heard it before.

She paused, wary. It could be that someone had docked on her island while she was in the house and that she hadn't heard the boat. Occasionally visitors came here without realizing it was private property, because it was so close to the Boundary Waters area and a camping ground. She waited, holding her breath in fear of the unknown.

ARMAND STOPPED in the small clearing to the right of the rock. The tune he had been whistling stuck in his throat when he spotted her, poised like a small fawn under the oak tree, sniffing danger yet unaware of its source. Faith. No, Hope. Hope, who looked so much like his love. She even acted very much as Faith had, all bravado outside, sweetness and melted sugar within. Despite her brashness, he could see the caring in her eyes. And the depth of emotion she had experienced this morning was more revealing than any of her words. So like his Faith.

Deliberately he broke the dry twig he held in his hand, drawing her startled gaze toward him.

At first she looked wary, then startled, then—although she probably didn't know it—pleasantly surprised to see him.

"Hello!" she called. "I thought you'd left."

One brow arched over a sardonic eye. "Where would I go?"

All she could do was guess. "Back to the rock?"

"Is that where you think I came from?" He stood at the edge of the picnic sheet, his head bent toward her, his stance relaxed. But she could feel the tension emanating from him.

She nodded. "I think so. Ever since I can remember I've thought that rock was alive. It seemed to know me, protect me, even care for me."

"And did you think that instead of it being just another rock, it could have been the soul of a man? A man who was very much in love?"

She lowered her eyes and stared down at the wine bottle. "Never," she said, covering her embarrassment by taking a sip of the wine. It warmed her throat and stomach pleasantly, making her feel flushed all over her body.

Armand sat in front of her on the sheet, stretching his long legs out on the grass and propping himself up on a bent elbow. He twiddled the broken twig in his hand. "Do not be embarrassed by true emotions and serious feelings, *chérie*. They are as important to the soul as real love," he said in his warm-as-whisky voice.

She smiled. "Spoken like a true Frenchman."

"And why not?" he countered. "I am a true Frenchman."

She bowed her head quickly, covering a smile with her hand. "You're quite right." The smile was harder to contain than she had thought. Every Frenchman she had ever met had held that same attitude. Why should he be any different?

"Why are you smiling? And why are you trying to hide it?"

Her eyes widened innocently. "Who, me?"

His jet-black brows drew together. "Is there someone else on the island?"

"Well, no," she admitted, then decided to continue. He might as well be brought up to date on current events. "But you see, there has long been a rumor that Frenchmen were autocratic and in love with love. They are also known to be chauvinistic."

"What is this, chauvinistic?"

"It's a phrase coined after one of your countrymen, Chauvin, a soldier who was totally devoted to Napoleon and his cause. The word has come to mean exaggerated patriotism, or exaggerated anything, in today's world. Women often use it when they refer to a man who believes he's supreme."

His dark frown grew darker. "I knew nothing of this," he said stiffly. "I have never heard of this Napoleon."

"No." She reached out to touch his hand, and he clasped hers. "I'm sorry, I forgot. He was a general, then the emperor of France in the very early eighteen hundreds. But you see, it's kind of hard to remember where you are in history compared to today." Her voice was gentle. "I'm afraid I only took a few history courses in university. And what I remember doesn't hold a candle to what I forgot." His hand was almost too warm, too strong, and she withdrew hers. His touch was erotic.

Again his eyes locked with hers, surprise showing there now. "You went to a university?"

She nodded. "Yes. The University of Maryland."

"Do all women go to this university, or just a few?"

She smiled. "About half the students are women in almost all the schools. At least during the first two years."

His brows rose in almost comic disbelief. "Women go to the same university as men?"

She nodded, her smile widening. "In the early days of America, women went to schools that were just for them. But soon that changed, and now we can even live with a man we like without having to marry him. As a matter of fact, many of my university friends lived with men while they were attending school. Women are no longer merely breeders. They can enjoy the same freedom, including sexual freedom, as men."

Armand sat up. "But that is wrong! How can those women face themselves without shame?"

Hope sat straighter. "What shame? Is it more shameful for the man to live with a woman—or the woman to live with the man?"

"Certainly that is apparent! The shame should be the woman's for allowing such a thing to happen. We have a word for women like that, and it is not nice," he stated autocratically.

"I can see we have a mutual education problem," she said slowly. "There is no shame in either circumstance. As long as they are above the age of consent, it's their choice and their business. No one else's."

He leaned back, and Hope could tell he was trying to digest these facts that, at least from his standpoint, were astounding. Finally he looked at her, his eyes probing. "You can read?"

She blinked at the change of subject, but answered. "Yes. Everyone is supposed to go to school until they're at least sixteen. Those who want can continue their education and then go on to college or university. Both women and men."

"How remarkable," he murmured, pondering that for a moment. Then he caught her eye. "You will read to me," he said, as if it was a foregone conclusion.

"Will I?" Could this man be Chauvin himself? Her voice was stiff with sarcasm. "And just what is it you want me to read to you?"

He waved a hand in the air. "Anything. Perhaps something that tells me what this world is like today." His gaze wavered, and she realized how insecure he was in this new world in which he found himself. "There are still books and such, are there not?"

"Yes. I think I even have some old newspapers and periodicals at the house."

He smiled delightedly. "Wonderful. That will do for a start."

"Oh," she said softly, almost too softly. Had he known her as well as he thought he did, he would have known that she was balking at his presumptions. "And why the hell can't you read them for yourself?"

"Do not swear. It is most unbecoming a lady. Even those who wear pantaloons," he admonished as he stared with a mixture of pleasure and disdain at the shapely limbs, so tightly encased in dark blue denim. He sighed deeply, as if his patience was almost at an end. "Because, *ma chérie*, I cannot read English well. And since you are English and speak English, I would assume you also read English. Am I not right?"

This time her smile was wide and warm, drawing one from him, as well. True wisdom must come with being more than two hundred years old. And she wouldn't bother arguing the point about her being English right now. He was coping with enough information. "Right."

"So, do you think you might fetch them and let me hear the news of today?" he continued patiently.

She waved her hand in the air as he had done. "Later. Right now I'm hungry."

His expression darkened again, but not another word was spoken as he reached for the bottle of wine and poured himself a glass and she munched on a peanut-butter-and-honey sandwich.

"Uggh!" he exclaimed, sputtering and slamming the glass onto the sheet. A torrent of French assaulted the air. Hope had the distinct feeling he was cursing her for something, but she couldn't make out for what. High-school French hadn't prepared her to say much more than the pen of my aunt is on the table.

She took another bite of her sandwich, watching him with a cautious eye to see if he would continue with his diatribe or give her an explanation.

"What is this? The urine of a goat? It is disgusting!" His expression underscored his words. "I thought you were drinking wine, but this liquid must be something new, a torture perhaps, or a cure for some dreaded disease!" He tried to decipher the label.

She swallowed her bite of sandwich, hiding her grin. "It's an inexpensive American wine. I'm not much of a wine drinker, so I find it adequate."

"Wine? Bah! This is nothing but sour, colored water! What is the name of the wine it is supposed to be disguising itself as?"

She turned the bottle around so it faced her. "It says it's a Chablis—"

"This isn't even a good enough table wine to serve the British!"

Finally she couldn't hold it in anymore and began chuckling. Her chuckles turned into laughter, then uncontrolled mirth.

"What is so funny?" he asked, exasperation etched on his features, and she knew he was wondering if she couldn't be just the slightest bit looney. She laughed even harder. He wasn't too far from wrong if that was what he was thinking!

"I'm sorry," she gasped when she finally caught her breath. "It's just that this is such a stupid situation! I'm supposed to be here to rest and regain my health. Instead, I find a ghost, even sit down to have a meal with him. And all we can do is argue about bad wine!"

Armand's face cleared, showing smug satisfaction. "Ahhh, so you agree with me about the wine!"

"The wine?" she sputtered, laughter bubbling out again. "Leave it to a man to try to prove his point, even when the world stops spinning!"

Gradually she calmed down to a giggle. He glanced at her, then reached for a sandwich. He examined the filling carefully before taking a wary bite. "Tell me. Do you not like men? Is that why you make such barbs about us?"

Her smile faded. "I'm not too fond of men right now. But if you're asking whether I prefer women, the answer is definitely no."

His frown disappeared. A bird twittered above. "I see. I did not think so, for when I held you in my arms, you responded."

"It was only an instinctive response, just like your body responding to holding me. You were warm, and I was cold and wet."

"You should not have noticed my response," he admonished sternly, a frown puckering his wide brow. "It is most unladylike."

"Oh, for heaven's sake," she said, feeling better now that he was the uncomfortable one.

His brows rose, but he made no reply. Hope reached for another half sandwich. So did Armand. He was hungry enough not to ask about the contents, even though he was obviously suspicious.

"What will happen next, do you think?" he asked; she paused before answering.

"I think we need to find out why you have never rested since, uh, since your demise."

"My death?"

"Yes," she said. "There must be a reason." She began digging through the picnic bag, finally finding the photos on the bottom. He had been so concerned earlier with the process of photography that she had forgotten to show him all the shots and to ask him about the event they represented. "Here. Study these and tell me what you remember." She held them out.

Armand stared at the photos, obviously reluctant.

She shook them. "They won't hurt you. Take them."

With careful deliberation he sat up, crossing his legs and sitting directly across from her. He wiped his hands on his pants, then reached for the photos. One by one, he studied them, his face becoming more set with every print. When he was through, he started over.

"Well? Do you remember anything?" she asked, excitement lacing her voice.

"Yes. I remember it all."

"Great!" She leaned forward expectantly. "Who were they? What did they want? Which one hurt you?"

A lean finger pointed to the man in high boots with a cape of furs tied around his shoulders. "This one is a trapper who lived more at Grand Portage than in the wild. His name was François Tourbet. This one—" he indicated the long-faced man next to Tourbet "—used to scout for Faith's father. He was a quiet man. Jacques Pillon. And this one—" He pointed to the one who stood alone at the side. "This is one of the cruelest men I have ever encountered. His name is Henri Houdon, and he used to tease the men constantly to urge them to fight. He hated everyone. Everyone except Captain Trevor. And sometimes I think he only tolerated the captain because Henri needed his goodwill so he would not be thrown out of the territory."

"Which one killed you?"

He looked at the photographs again, laying them carefully on the sheet, then rearranging them, just as Hope had done earlier. "There is no picture of the murder," Armand muttered, as if to himself. Then he stared out toward the rock, his mind obviously turning back to that hideous scene. "I was so impatient. I had traveled to Port Huron disguised as a voyageur, because the French soldiers were not welcome there. I had hired Jacques Pillon at Port Huron to guide me to my brother at Fort Francis, his last known location. We stopped at Grand Portage, only to find out that the Ojibwa tribe was at war with another tribe. Jacques picked up the other two men because they knew the territory by land, and instead of following the Pigeon River to Fort Francis, we had to skirt the tribes by going overland in a circular route. We came south from Grand Portage and began swinging up when we came to this island, staying on it so the roaming Indians could not reach us easily. It was here that I buried my small brass chest and changed into my uniform. From this point on we were in the territory France controlled. However, the chest was too cumbersome to carry, and I did not trust my fellow travelers. I had a journal, and a miniature of Faith in that chest."

He closed his eyes for a moment, and when he opened them again they held a bleakness that wrenched at Hope's soul. "I had been trying to talk my brother into returning home and taking up his duties as head of the household. But he refused. I finally gave up, and we returned by the same path we had taken before. When we reached this island, the others camped down below, and I came up here. I was getting ready to dig up my chest when they came upon me."

Hope's brow furrowed. "Why would they want the chest? It doesn't seem to have much value to me."

He continued as if she hadn't spoken. "I had the key on my person. A large ivory key bound in brass. I treasured the chest because it contained my wedding gift for Faith. I was going to present her with it when we reached the ship and the captain performed the wedding ceremony." His expression clouded with the darkness of bitter memories washing over him. "She was my life, my love. Everything."

A lump formed in Hope's throat as she watched the handsome man in front of her crying quietly, tears coursing unstemmed down his cheeks. "She was everything to me," he whispered. "The sun would not shine if she was not near." He was lost in his memories of a love so strong that, hoping to find her again, he hadn't been able to leave this earth when he should have.

She cleared her throat. "Why would they want a miniature of Faith?"

He looked at her as if seeing her for the first time since he had begun speaking. He smiled, a sad, bittersweet gesture that touched her heart. "Not the painting. They wanted my journal, knowing that it would be harmful to Faith's father and themselves. Things were not right at the trading posts the voyageurs were using. Men were cheating France as well as England. And they knew I had probably kept a record of it."

"So that was their motive for killing you?" Hope leaned forward, her hand touching his as if to encourage him to keep talking.

"*Oui.* That, and the fact that somehow they knew Faith and I were to leave in four nights' time, when I reached Port Huron." His face twisted in pain. "But how did they know? No one knew, except Faith and myself and the man who was to help us navigate the lakes and rivers."

"Perhaps the navigator got scared. Perhaps he went to the captain."

"No." Armand's tone was definite. "He wanted to get away as badly as we did. His wife was with child and waiting for him in New York. They were to open a bakery together. He was so excited, so happy to be leaving the wilderness and returning to civilization, if you could call the muddy streets of New York that."

Hope remembered her last visit to New York. If Armand could only see it now! "Could Faith's father have badgered her into telling him? After all, he was her father."

He shook his head. "No. She was frightened of him, I know, but she wanted to leave with me as much as I wanted her to come. She loved me. I *know* it!"

Hope's heart went out to him. Despite what he said, she knew he now doubted Faith's love. In the beginning she'd been willing to believe that Faith had not loved him enough, but now she wasn't sure. Was it wishful thinking on her part, wanting to believe in a love more real to her than Romeo and Juliet?

"Do you think they found the chest?"

He shrugged. "I do not think so. The ivory key was the only thing they could have taken." He caressed her with his indigo eyes. "Does it matter? It is all over now."

"Of course it matters! If they found the chest, then they got what they wanted. If they didn't find the chest, then they must have spent the rest of their lives looking over their shoulders, wondering who would discover it and accuse them of whatever it was you knew they were doing."

"They were stealing furs and using the money to buy land in the east. They had formed a company into which they funnelled the funds; then an attorney in England bought the land outside the colonies. They were going to set up their own country."

"Well." She sat back, satisfied. "At least you know their plans didn't work. The colonies fought against the British and won independence. Then the land was divided into areas we call states and each one governs itself under the protection of the United States of America."

Armand looked interested, but she could tell she had mystified him again. "But who is the ruler? Is he English, French or Spanish?"

"New France, as you called it, is now called Canada, and is ruled by a prime minister. America is governed by presidents, and they're all American."

"American? Are they Indians?"

"No," she said, chuckling. "Americans. People born in America, or who have lived here long enough to become citizens."

"Are there so many, then? Even in my time British women gave birth to British subjects." His brow was furrowed, as if he couldn't grasp her words and make sense of them.

"I'll tell you what. Tomorrow I'll bring a history book as well as the newspapers. There must be a dozen at the farmhouse. Maybe they will explain better than I can." She began repacking the picnic basket, realizing for the first time that the late sunset was putting on quite a show. They had spent most of the afternoon and early evening talking. "I'll be back in the morning," she promised, more to herself than to him. "And I'll bring a few provisions, so I won't have to keep walking up and down that damn hill."

"Do not curse, it is—"

Before he could complete his sentence, she finished it for him. "I know . . . it's unladylike." She chuckled, wondering what it would be like to take him away from the island and into civilization. Talk about culture shock! He'd probably go into cardiac arrest! "I'll try to remember, but it won't be easy."

"*Merci,*" he murmured with the trace of a smile, standing so she could fold the plastic-lined sheet.

"You're welcome," she answered automatically, her mind on other things. Where would he sleep tonight? On the ground, floating in the air, curled up by the rock? Where? She handed him the folded material. "Here. I'm leaving this with you. Just in case."

"In case of what?"

"In case you need it," she said impatiently.

"Do you think I will need to eat again while you are gone?"

"No, but—but where will you sleep?" She finally got out, feeling extremely foolish until she saw his expression. *He* hadn't thought about that at all!

"You may have a point, *chérie.* I have no idea where—or if—I will sleep. Or even if I will be here when dawn breaks." He smiled, and the glow warmed her insides. "But we shall see, no?"

"We shall see, yes," she answered. "Meanwhile, try to think of other things, things that could help us solve the mystery of why you're still here. Maybe we can put our heads together and come up with an answer."

"I would love to put our two heads together, *chérie.* It would be most, uh, stimulating. Yes?"

"And you're supposed to be a respectable ghost!" she admonished. "Respectable ghosts don't go around making advances!"

"How do you know?" His eyes twinkled. "You told me I was your first ghost."

"Men! You're all the same! You profess to love Faith, but you'd tumble in the hay with the first girl who comes along!"

He stiffened as if she had hit him. "You are right. I do love Faith. I was pretending, for just a moment, that she was you. I am sorry if I hurt you."

She knew she should have let up, but some perverse demon in her wouldn't allow it. "Then just remember who I am, please. Let's solve your problem so you can get back to wherever it is that you're supposed to be, and I can get on with my own life."

"*Oui*," he muttered, turning his back to her. "We shall do just that, *Mademoiselle* Hope. Good evening." And he strolled away, disappearing behind the boulder and leaving her alone.

The instant he disappeared, she felt lonely.

4

A FOGGY MIST floated eerily a few feet above the calm water. Puffs of white caught in the pine trees like angel hair, tugging at the branches as if asking to be allowed to float freely wherever the soft breeze carried them. It all seemed so achingly familiar to him.

He huddled in a fetal bundle under the waterproof sheet, and watched the slim form of the woman run down the path toward the small boat tied to the pier. Where was she going? There was no use calling out or running to her. He could not go far without hitting that invisible wall, and he doubted she would hear his call. His fingers itched to comb through her long, almost waist-length hair and cradle her head against his chest.

The emotions that thought provoked stiffened his body in protest. His hands clenched the sheet tighter. But he didn't have the power to eliminate those thoughts. An almost overwhelming sadness pervaded his very being. *Mon Dieu!* He was a ghost. A ghost! It did not matter that he felt more a man than a specter. Fact was fact. He was out of his time, his past, his own life . . . caught up in the whirling, confusing tide of the future. And he did not even know what his future was!

His friends and relatives, as well as his enemies, were gone, leaving him totally alone but for a woman who looked like his Faith. A woman who swore that she and others like her were liberated. What did that mean?

Aside from being allowed to run around naked, what else could she do in this new, modern society? He had seen the pictures—the photographs—but he was not sure what they were for. He had seen the contraption she called a zipper, but besides closing her jacket, what else did it do? It looked like a substitute for buttons. There was nothing new in that; all it did was change something that worked fine before. He couldn't comprehend all the differences Hope had pointed out.

Her small boat made a strange, hollow rumble that echoed through the stillness of dawn. He squinted, noticing for the first time that there was a contraption on the stern that was making the noise. Hope steered away from the snug harbor and headed toward the far shore and another dock. The boat moved quickly, much faster than fourteen voyageurs could paddle their *canots de maîtres* up the accessways in search of furs.

His brow creased in frustration. There was so much he did not know and could not understand! Had he frightened her so that she had decided to leave the island permanently? He did not think so, but how could he be certain?

He rested his head on his knees and shut his eyes tightly. Even though he had been so cavalier with Hope yesterday, he was scared to death. Afraid to see the past or to look into the future. Oddly, most of all, he was afraid of losing Hope.

No matter what she believed, he couldn't feel the way he did toward her if Hope Langston wasn't really his Faith, could he? His love. His life. No man would be drawn to a woman just because she looked like the woman he loved. He had to feel the compatibility of souls also.

A low moan was torn from his throat, but no one else was there to hear it resounding through the crisp morning air.

HOPE RACED the car engine as she headed toward Two Harbors, a small town just down the highway from the dock that took her to her island. She needed to be alone for a little while in order to digest everything that had happened. She simply had to make some kind of sense of all this or admit she was going bonkers.

But sense wasn't a factor to be introduced conveniently into this particular set of circumstances. In fact, it was the last thing she could use as glue in this whole episode. A ghost? On her island? Impossible! Especially one more than two hundred years old, and just as arrogant as any men she might encounter today. She couldn't control the grin that teased the corners of her mouth. Some things didn't change with the passage of time, and apparently the male ego was one of them.

But why was Armand here? Something had happened to make him—or his spirit—remain stuck in time. But what? And why now? She didn't know enough about the topic to be able to give an educated guess. Next stop, the library. Certainly there had to be books on ghosts, or reincarnation, or whatever it was that Armand was involved in! Right now she didn't have a clue as to whether it was the violence of his death or his intense love for Faith that had brought him back. Perhaps it was something else entirely.

In any case, there had to be *something* that would lay him to rest. Could the secret lie within the buried chest where Faith's miniature was, or was it the ivory key that opened it? Or finding Faith's grave and chanting some

magic words over it? Or Armand's grave? She didn't
know, and obviously neither did Armand. But her loss
of sleep last night had confirmed what they both already knew. She had to find some answers, and this
morning was as good a time as any. Besides, she needed
so many things to make their lives a little easier while
they were working this problem through.

So far she didn't have any answers, but felt confident she would find *something*.

They'd just have to try one thing at a time and see
what happened. Hopefully some research at the library would provide answers to her questions—and
give her the answers she needed.

Only when she reached the small, picturesque town
did she realize that she needed bigger facilities. A bigger library, bigger stores, more sources of information.

But the trip to Duluth would have to wait for another day. Right now, she would make do with the local library and at least get her shopping done.

She walked the main street browsing through the
many outfitters' shops, where anything anyone could
ever need for camping in the Boundary Waters Canoe
Area was for sale or rent. Between the rows of build-
ings, she occasionally glimpsed the vast waters of Lake
Superior lapping at the shore and docks. On any other
day, she would have strolled the length of town and
loved the slow-paced atmosphere.

But today she had to hurry... there was so much to
do!

HOPE GAVE A SIGH as she reached into the trunk for the
last paper bag. Her purchases were even more exten-

sive than she had planned. The trunk, the back seat, and even part of the front were crowded with packages and groceries. It had taken several trips to get everything into the small boat.

She had bought everything she thought they might need for the next couple of weeks to make Armand's time on the island more comfortable. What food she had at the house was supposed to have lasted a couple of weeks, and had been bought for only one person. There was certainly not enough left to satisfy *his* appetite. Ghost or not, he ate like the robust man he appeared to be.

As she guided her boat toward the island, the late-afternoon sun hung like a bright orange ball just above the treetops making the tall conifers blaze. Despite her tiredness, the sunset was too breathtakingly spectacular to ignore.

A more immediate attention-getter, though, was the sound of someone shouting her name. She turned and searched the island's shoreline. Armand stood about a hundred yards from the dock, waving his arms to attract her attention. His white shirt was open at the throat, revealing the edge of a nest of dark hair that no doubt covered his chest. His dusty Hessian boots looked inky black from the distance. The dark gold pants outlined his strong, pillared legs. He must have been tall for his time, she mused, guessing he was a few inches under six feet. No one could have looked more solid and less like a ghost than he did.

Swerving the small craft toward him, she watched him grow larger as she approached. A small thrill of happiness shivered through her as she realized he was still there. She hadn't had enough dealings with ghosts to know for sure that he would still be around. She had only hoped.

His smile was dazzling as she shut down the motor and glided into shore. Leaning over and hooking his strong fingers over the edge of the bow, he hauled the boat into the sloping shore. "I did not think you would return," he said, his indigo eyes riveting her to the seat.

"I had some shopping to do," she replied. "But what happened to you? I thought you couldn't get off the hill?"

His eyes darted away, but not before she saw the pain etched there. "I still cannot, but it seems that I am able to reach the water on this side. On the opposite side I can walk three rods into the water. Then I hit the same wall." A heartbreakingly sad smile twisted his lips. "At least I know where I can bathe."

"Have you followed it all the way around? Perhaps there's a hole somewhere!" Her voice echoed the excitement her uplifted face revealed.

He shook his head, his dark hair catching the last scarlet rays of the sun. "It is no use, my sweet. I cannot climb over it, nor can I swim under it. I know. I have been trying ever since you left early this morning."

She looked behind her to where the supplies were stacked. "Then help me get this stuff up the hill. I've got a few surprises for you."

Both brows shot up. "For me? Presents?"

She laughed, a clear bright sound that drifted across the treetops. He wasn't aware that sound had been a long time coming; until him, there had been no reason to laugh, no one to laugh with. "Yes, presents," she said gaily as she threw him one of the larger bags. "Things that will make it easier for you while you're . . ."

His voice was soft, his glance even softer as he looked down at her, the bag held in his arms. "While I'm still here?"

"Yes." She reached for another bag, ignoring the twinge of emptiness that touched her with that thought.

She filled his arms with packages, then picked up a bunch herself. Companionably they walked up the almost overgrown path to the top of the knoll, Hope just behind Armand, watching the muscles of his back as they stretched with every step. For a ghost he was in remarkably good shape. For a man he was absolutely terrific.

"So, what is all this?" he asked, dropping the packages on the dappled ground beneath the large oak.

She groaned with relief as she let go of her load, then sat down and began burrowing through the larger bags. With a satisfied grin, she held up her bulky find. "Aha!"

Armand's eyes narrowed warily. "And what is that lumpy object?"

Hope examined the fabric, then looked at him, stifling a smile. "It's a down-filled sleeping bag. One of the best on the market." She undid the string and allowed it to unroll. "See?"

Armand hunkered down, feeling the material, turning it over in his strong capable hands. "A zip-pier? Is that right?" he asked, playing with its stem.

"Yes, a zipper. You crawl into it, and then you zip it up and it keeps you warm."

"And very comfortable?"

She nodded emphatically. "Very."

The smile that creased his mouth and indented his cheeks suffused her with warmth. She stared up at him, mesmerized. *"Merci bien, ma petite,"* he said softly, touching her soft cheek with his finger and sending a bolt of lightning down her spine.

Her lips barely moved in reply. "You're welcome."

His gaze was riveted on her mouth, his whole body drawn toward her as he balanced on the balls of his feet. "How sweet you are," he murmured before bending down and gently capturing her parted lips. His kiss was warm and soft, yet firm. Heated brandy coursed through her bloodstream as his mouth moved over hers to capture the very essence of her.

She hugged one end of the sleeping bag, her fingers gripping the cloth as if to tear it. Electric responses rushed through her system, forcing her to focus completely on the soft caress of his mouth.

When he eased away, she trembled from the chill his absence brought. Her eyes were half-closed, and her pulse throbbed visibly in the small indentation at the base of her throat.

"You are very special to think of me," he murmured, drawing his hand away from her neck.

She cleared her throat and pasted a smile on her lips, one that she was sure looked even more stupid than it felt. "I can't have a frozen ghost on my hands. What would I do with you then?"

He grinned, relaxing once more. It seemed strange, but for a moment she would have sworn he was as moved by their kiss as she had been. "Keep your food from spoiling?"

Her eyes rounded. "The food! It's still down at the dock!" She jumped up and ran for the path. "And so is the rest of the equipment!"

She didn't even glance back to see if he was following. She needed the time to sort out her own emotions before confronting his. She was sure they both knew that the kiss had been more than it should have been.

"I also have some Levi's and a shirt for you!" she called over her shoulder. "They should be more comfortable than what you have on!"

"What is this . . . Levi's?"

"Blue jeans!" She laughed, imagining his look when he saw them.

"I do not want them," he said, coming up behind her to take some of the bags out of her arms. He retraced his steps up the hill. "I have an excellent tailor. He is the only one I trust."

"You'll love them," she promised. "Besides, your tailor isn't here, so these will have to do."

"We shall see," he said, but his voice assured her that his mind was closed on the matter.

Twenty minutes later, she knew he was right. She tried to stifle the laughter that begged to escape from her throat, only barely controlling herself. The lightweight plaid-flannel shirt she'd bought him fit too tightly around his powerful chest. The sleeves hung beyond his hands. But the jeans... The jeans were even funnier.

He stood in front of her, disgust all over his handsome face. "I do not know what Americans must think of themselves to wear such a garment," he muttered, staring at his legs.

"If you'd pull them down a bit so they ride on your hips instead of your waist, it might help," she said, still trying very hard to hide her laughter.

"Hips?" One eyebrow elevated. "When I do that, the fabric in the *derrière* bags down." He turned around to show her. "And this fabric is very rough, very coarse.

This is made for the peasants who work in the fields, am I not correct?"

"No," she gurgled. "It's every American's favorite leisure wear."

He began to undo the buttons, anxious to shed the jeans. "I *knew* the French had better sense than to design something so distasteful," he said, with a look that spoke volumes.

That did it. She dipped forward in laughter, the musical sound echoing over the water. She heard another grunt of disgust from Armand, but couldn't begin to answer. By the time she had caught her breath, he was returning from the other side of the boulder, where he had changed his clothes in privacy. "Did you enjoy my discomfort, Hope?" His nose looked pinched around the nostrils.

"Please." She reached out her hand to him. "Try to understand. Everyone wears them, even in France. I just didn't know the size to buy so they would fit correctly. I wasn't laughing at you, I was seeing our clothing through your eyes, and it was very funny. I don't blame you for not wanting to wear them."

He stared at her hard, as if making up his mind about something. Slowly his smile began to peep out at her, and the familiar warmth soothed her. "I think I knew that," he said. "Since you are wearing them, I realized that you just wanted to help me to have something that is also comfortable for you. But you see, my Hope, your figure is much more, uh, pliable for this garment than mine. If you do not mind, I will continue to wear what feels comfortable to me. I can wash my clothes in the lake."

"You're right," she smiled back. "Maybe next time I'll try a different size."

"There will be no next time, Hope," he stated imperiously. "I will wear what I have and be done with it."

She grinned. He must have really hated them. "Very well," she said.

"Good. Now let us review the rest of the items."

By the time they had everything unpacked, it was nearly dark. With a minimum of words, they erected the tent she had bought, placing it in front of a small stand of aspens. She unpacked a gas lantern, filled it, and hung it on a small tree beside the tent.

"There," she said, slapping her hands against her now-dusty jeans. "That's much better."

"Better than what?" Armand asked, his brow furrowing.

"Better than nothing."

"A sleeping bag down is better than anything. This is soft."

"A down sleeping bag," she corrected. "It's filled with goose down."

Some of the stiffness left him. "I must try to learn better English, no? Then this is like a *couvre-pied*, a featherbed that we have at home, except this material is much different."

"It's a man-made fiber called nylon," she explained, grinning. It was both fun and frustrating to explain things that she had always taken for granted. "And speaking of man-made, did France have libraries when you lived there? Places that you could go to and rent books to read?"

He shook his head. "Only the wealthy could afford the cost of a library in their home." He shrugged. "And why would the poor want to rent books? They were not taught to read and write, so it would only be paper and board to clean and take care of."

"It's different now. Now there are presses, and hundreds of books are printed each month. The public library carries most of them, or can get ahold of them. This way people get to read whatever interests them."

"There are so many books, now? But why? There is not that much information to absorb in order to live in this world."

"Because this way everyone can read about what interests them the most. I'm telling you this because I want to explain that I went to the public library today and looked up some information for us," she said before getting to the heart of the purpose of her trip. "I found some information on ghosts and made some notes. If anything, I'm more confused than ever."

"Why?"

"According to the books I've gone through, it seems that ghosts come back for a multitude of reasons. It can be because of an undying love, or to fulfill a purpose that was not completed in his lifetime, especially vengeance for crimes against him. It also might be an improper burial." She refused to look at him, choosing instead to pretend to read her notes, although she knew them by heart.

With his finger under her chin, he lifted her head so their eyes could meet. "And what do you think of all this?"

"I don't know."

"Hmm," he teased. "I would say that it is too late to bury me properly. We don't even know what my murderers did with me."

She winced.

"And Faith is gone. Since you swear that you are not Faith and I am sure that when she died she was properly buried, I would say that I am too late for undying love."

"Don't joke, Armand! I'm trying to help you!"

He shrugged, dropping his hand from her chin. "I do not know what else to do. I do not understand, either, but I know that we cannot change some of those things. I suggest that we try to change the things we can and not worry about what has already been done and cannot be undone."

"Like what?"

"For example, my original goal was to get back to Port Huron, and to Faith. Since I cannot leave this island, then I do not see how we can do anything concerning this purpose. But since three men were involved with the robbing of my possessions, perhaps my being here was something to do with them."

"You mean that instead of returning for Faith, you were brought back because of the three men?"

He nodded. "*Oui.* After all, I am stuck on the very hill where I was killed. No?"

"Yes," she said slowly, digesting that idea. "Or it could be because you want your possessions back. That was mentioned in one of the books I read."

"Perhaps."

"Or . . ." She hesitated, then rushed on. "It could be that you lost your way to heaven."

"Heaven?" He rolled his eyes skyward, and she chuckled, relaxing a little. The idea of sitting around and discussing Armand's death was just a little on the bizarre side!

"Heaven, the happy hunting grounds, Elysian Fields, Valhalla. One of the articles said that ghosts are yearning for those places but are being somehow blocked."

His brow furrowed. "Interesting. But not conclusive. How would one help a ghost find his heaven?"

"A séance?"

"Bah! It is too much like hocus-pocus, Hope. I doubt that there are very many people who can do such things. In my time there were people who swore they could speak to the dead, but they were hucksters—taking money from innocents in exchange for false hope."

"Okay, let's say we eliminate that. What next?"

"See if there is any information on the men? Find out if they stole my possessions? That would seem the logical choice of action."

"Right." She grinned. How could someone be so objective about his own death, even making the discussion fun?

"What else did you do while you were gone?" he asked, as though he'd heard her thoughts.

"I brought something for you to read." She burrowed into the smaller pile of bags she had yet to go through, pulling out some old French magazines. "These were in a used-book store, and I thought you might enjoy them."

He flipped through the pages, stopping at the printed words almost as often as he stared at the pictures of cars, jewelry and fashions. "This language looks like French, but it is different," he muttered.

"Really?" She looked over his arm and stared at the printed words. "Has it really changed so much?"

"I think so, yes," he murmured, scanning what was obviously an ad for a watch. "It is truly a miracle to wear a clock on the wrist."

"Oh," she said breezily. "It's not that great. In a few years they'll even have TVs to wear on wrists."

"What is a teevee?"

She wanted to reach up and smooth away his confused frown with her fingertips. Instead she clenched her hand into a fist. "Never mind." She turned away and rooted through the rest of the packages.

A night owl swooped from one tree branch to another; the echo of its hooting surrounded them.

"Tell me more," he demanded autocratically, dropping the magazine onto the sleeping bag. "I can read when you are gone."

"Where am I going?" She glanced over her shoulder at him, surprised at his tone. He sounded almost impatient.

He stood with his hands low on his hips, most of his weight on one booted foot. "To your home, of course. But before you go, I need to know more. I need to understand."

She sat back on her heels. "There are a few things I need to know, too. In fact, I bought a tape recorder. I want you to tell me everything you know about the three men who attacked you, as well as about Faith's father. That way I might be able to understand this puzzle and help you to find your way back to . . . wherever it is you're supposed to be. We'll solve the puzzle, and then you can be on your way."

"How do you know it will work?"

"I don't, but it's our only chance." Her eyes locked with his. "Faith might be waiting for you somewhere."

He stared into the darkness. "Do you think that is so?"

She cocked her head, wondering why he was so distant all of a sudden. Didn't he love Faith enough to want to find her? Her confusion must have shown on her face, because his expression softened.

"I am just wondering if Faith wants me to find her. Perhaps I am here because she did not love me enough?"

"Have some hope," she said before she realized her own words. She waved her hand through the air as if erasing her words. "Never mind. We'll talk about it later." She stood and stretched, ready to leave. Last night, sleep had been elusive, and today's activity had already taken its toll. She still didn't have all her strength back, yet here she was pretending to be Wonder Woman. She zipped up her light jacket, pretending to be chilled.

Those indigo eyes bored into her like drills. "I am hungry," he said. It was stated flatly, as if a banquet would drop into his lap upon saying the words.

Irritation laced her voice; the man was perfectly capable of feeding himself. "Fine. In one of those bags is a large bucket of fried chicken, along with corn on the cob and mashed potatoes and biscuits. Help yourself."

"You are leaving?"

"Yes." She turned and headed for the path toward the bottom of the hill and home. "I'm tired. Good night."

His own reply was soft as a breeze as it drifted down the slope to her, but his meaning was crystal clear. "You are not afraid to sleep down there by yourself?"

She peeked over her shoulder and caught the small smile tugging at the corners of his chiseled lips. "Why should I be? The ghost is up here—landlocked."

"Huh! There are worse things than ghosts, my Hope." His voice still carried down to her, even though his tone was low. "You should sleep up here where I will be able to protect you."

"I don't need protection.'

"But what if you did? I would not be able to reach you." His brows edged upward. "The invisible wall, remember?"

"I remember very well. I'll see you tomorrow," she said, dismissing his offer. "I'll be recording our conversation, so be ready."

"Good night, my Hope." She could hear the double meaning in his voice.

"Good night." She waved a hand and continued trudging toward the base of the hill and to her bed.

It wasn't until after midnight that she realized he'd been right. She should have stayed at the top of the hill with him, for her house and bed were the loneliest places on earth....

THE FOLLOWING MORNING Armand stood just below the crest of the hill and waited for Hope to appear. He leaned against the rugged bark of the tallest pine, his eyes trained on the small two-storied house just below. From what he could see on the outside, it was not much different from the rural-style clapboard homes he had seen being built in Montreal or New York or Boston, or any of the growing cities in the New World.

Except this dwelling held his Hope.

He had slept comfortably all night in his sleeping-down bag, the tent keeping off most of the night-chilled wind. He had read—or tried to read—most of the magazines before his eyes agreed they would stay shut in slumber.

Rambling thoughts had turned his brain topsy-turvy, but at least he had come up with one thought that would not change no matter how much light he poured upon it.

He had loved Faith with all his heart. Nothing could change that love. For him to be as drawn to Hope as he had been to Faith, his feelings must have some basis besides her appearance. He just did not know what that basis was.

Where in the world was she right now? She had promised to be here in the morning. Frustration at not being able to reach her rose in his throat like bile. Two feet away, the invisible wall held him tighter than any prison, far better than any stockade. He was a prisoner, and he could see no way out. Not that he hadn't tried. All day yesterday he had followed the invisible wall, banging at it, kicking, even diving to the bottom of the lake trying to find an opening. There was none.

He clenched his fists in frustration. Damn her! Did she not know that he was waiting for her, wishing to see her, to laugh with her, to be angry with her?

He picked up a stone that was by his foot and tossed it toward the house, waiting for it to bounce off the invisible wall.

It did not.

He picked up another, weighed it in his hand, then threw that one. It landed near Hope's doorstep, skipping and rolling until it bounced against the small steps that led to the back door.

He threw another and another. And another. If a rock, several rocks that were thrown by his hand, went through the barrier, why couldn't he? Was he not fast enough? Perhaps speed was the thing.

Testing first, he pulled off his boot and threw it toward the back door with all his might. It landed on the steps after skidding through the gravel. A war whoop escaped his throat and echoed around the island.

Backing up the hill, he kept his eye on the pine sapling near the spot where he knew the wall began. His heart pumped excitedly at the thought of breaking through and reaching Hope. As soon as he had enough space for a running leap, he began to propel his body forward with all the energy he could muster, dashing down the hill at breakneck speed. The moment he heard the back screen door open, he hit the wall.

HOPE'S HEART was in her mouth as she saw Armand fling himself at the wall, moving as fast as a runner could. Her breath caught when he hit the ground to lie unmoving at the very spot they had marked earlier as the boundary for the barrier that kept him away from the bottom of the hill.

Before she even knew it, she was moving. Stumbling over something on her porch, she looked down and realized it was a dusty piece of leather. Armand's boot!

Grabbing it, she ran as fast as she could toward the body lying on the hillside, her breath stinging her lungs. She passed through the wall and knelt at his side, reaching instinctively for the pulse at the base of his throat.

It was strong and regular against her fingertips, belying any fears that ghosts weren't alive in some sense. Thick, dark lashes any girl would kill for contrasted with the bronze of his cheeks.

Sitting on the ground, she propped her chin on her knees and waited for him to come to his senses. Obviously, the big lug had decided to defy his own boundaries, to no avail. Stubborn. Arrogant. Handsome.

Her hand stole out to test the texture of his hair; it felt just as she'd thought it would. Her fingertips darted down to seek the whiskery hair of his sideburns. It was then she realized that his hair, usually caught in a low ponytail tied back with a length of rawhide, was now loose and flowing, more luxuriant than most women's. She combed her fingers through it, loving it, touching it over and over as if she were acting out a mantra. Her wrist touched his neck, and her hands quickly followed suit, drifting down to stroke the curve where neck met shoulder. All the strength of that spot was under her palm: his muscle tone was superb.

Then she realized that his penetrating eyes were open and he was staring at her face, just as she was staring at his form. She stiffened.

"Do not stop now, *ma petite*," he said in a sensual whisper that rattled her nerves.

"You're awake. Do you feel all right?"

"A little sore. My shoulder hurts." She snatched her hand away as if he were aflame. "The other one."

"Oh."

"Do I look like a prince under a spell, as in those fairy stories my *grandmère* used to tell me?" His voice was still low, caressing her, calming her, keeping her from fleeing.

"Yes," she said huskily.

"Does that mean I get a kiss to wake me up?"

"You're already awake."

He closed his eyes. "Then I will go back to sleep until you kiss me."

"You'll be a long time waiting." She spoke louder to break the spell he was weaving, but it didn't work. He didn't bat one long, dark lash.

She waited.

Finally she leaned over to study his closed lids, then his mouth. Her lips were trembling as they brushed his. He was so solid, and warm enough, and very, very sexy. Her lips brushed his again, then again.

His arms stole around her shoulders and he drew her close, preventing her mouth from escaping the sweet pressure of his. His tongue darted, daring her to respond in kind. Slowly she came alive, wanting . . . no, needing his kiss as much as she needed to breathe.

She felt the rise and fall of his powerful chest, and a heartbeat that grew stronger and more erratic with every passing moment. Even so, she knew she could pull away at any time; he wouldn't try to stop her from withdrawing.

But his knowledge of her body, her traitorous, sensual body, was the other reason she remained locked in his arms. He seemed to know her better than she knew herself. When one large hand cupped her breast as if it was something precious and fragile, she moaned.

His lips slid away from hers to travel to the curve of her throat and taste her there. Then he dipped his head toward her shoulder, nipping her soft flesh with strong white teeth.

She couldn't quite catch her breath and she didn't care. Her head was spinning from his touch, her heartbeat was as erratic as his. Her hands sought the strength of his shoulders as if needing an anchor on a stormy sea. Her fingertips dug into the muscles of his upper arms, trailing down to his elbow only to find their way to his chest and the strong definition of muscle there.

"Mon amour," he whispered, his voice raspy with need. He inhaled deeply of her scent, a mixture of flowers and soap and an indefinable quality that was pure Hope. "My love."

As nothing else had, his words broke the spell. She chuckled nervously, drawing away. "My goodness," she said lightly as she pulled her long hair away from her face and looked everywhere but into his eyes. "I never thought I'd have to give mouth-to-mouth resuscitation to a ghost," she laughed.

"What?" He frowned, his hands still holding her arms lightly.

"Never mind," she said quietly, her brain still refusing to function beyond the level of instinct. She pulled farther away and began to fuss with her hair to disguise the tremors in her hands and keep him from noticing the trembling in her body.

"Fai—" He stopped, sensing instantly the hurt in her eyes as she was startled into looking at him. "Hope," he amended, his hands wrapping around her arms once more. "Tell me what it is."

Instead, she stood up, towering over him as she stared down. "Put your boots on and meet me at the top of the hill. We have work to do if we're ever going to get you where you're supposed to be, with Faith. I'll be along in a few minutes." And with that she spun around and hurried down the hill, as if she believed he could follow her.

But he couldn't, and it only added to his frustration.

5

HOPE PLACED the cassette recorder on the ground between them, then crossed her legs Indian-fashion. "Okay," she began, "I'm going to ask you questions, and you tell me as much as you can. Anything might be a clue without your realizing it, so just talk your heart out."

But his devilish smile knocked the journalistic business right out of her head and left her with butterflies in her stomach, instead. "Now that I understand what the machine does, I will be more than happy to accommodate you. It pleasures me to know you will be listening to my voice even when you are not with me."

"Typical male," she muttered. Trying to focus her attention on the recorder, she turned it on. "Okay, now. Where was Faith born?"

"She was born in England and raised in New York. Her father was in the British Army, recently stationed at the fort on Lake Huron. When her mother died, she followed him out there, taking the route from Montreal through Sault Ste. Marie. She was accompanied by two other women—servants."

"How did her mother die?" Hope's voice was clear and unemotional, as if she were interviewing someone she didn't know at all. She only wished she could convince her pulse of that.

"Her mother died of the fever, I believe. She was a very ill woman all her life. Despite her condition, Captain Trevor brought her to this barbarian country, leaving her in New York City with a twelve-year-old Faith, even though his wife pleaded with him to allow her to die in England. But he thought it would be better to have her here, thus demonstrating the loyalty of his family and helping to entertain other British officers' wives. He should have allowed her to stay in England until his tours in New York and then Port Huron in the Northwest Territory were over." His voice held a note of disgust for the man.

"How old was Faith when this happened?"

"Sixteen."

"And how old was she when you met her?"

His brows rose. "The same age. I met her the day after she arrived at the Port Huron. I was pretending to be a French voyageur—a trapper—until I reached the French-occupied territory. Until then, the uniform had a—how do you say?—tendency to get in my way. The British dogs can strike a Frenchman in the back at night and not soil their honor."

Nothing registered except his first statement. "Sixteen? You were in love with a sixteen-year-old girl?" Hope's voice rose incredulously. "How old were you?"

Armand's eyes turned puzzled. "I am thirty-one."

"A thirty-one-year-old world-weary soldier in love with a giggling teenager?" Hope forgot that the tape recorder was still running, that she was supposed to be conducting an interview and should remain objective. All that went by the wayside in the face of her emotions of the moment.

"Yes." His eyes were even more puzzled than before.

"I don't believe it," she said disgustedly. "That's practically obscene."

"How so?" he asked, as intrigued by her reaction as he was hurt by it.

Hope stopped, remembering she was not talking to a man of her own times. "Faith was just a child," she tried to explain in a more subdued tone, ignoring the stab of pain that seared through her when she imagined Armand and a teenager together.

"No," he interjected firmly. "Faith was a woman, born and bred for the position of wife and mother. She would have been married to a British officer her father had chosen for her, but her mother was ill. She could cook, clean, sew, and take care of a husband and children. She had been expertly trained for that purpose all her life. What is so wrong about it?"

"You were too old for her!" Hope hurled the words at him, impatient with his lack of understanding. "She was just a child!"

He shook his head. "No. She was a woman. She was ready to be bedded, ready to bear children. What else would she do? Become a governess for someone else's children?" In bewilderment, he shook his head again. "No, she was just right for me. I was ready to settle down and take up the responsibilities of a wife and nursery, and she was of the right age to give me as many children as I deemed necessary." He stared over Hope's shoulder for a moment as sadness settled over him; then slowly, he brought his eyes back into focus with hers. "Most women I know marry between the ages of fifteen and eighteen. It is the only way for a man to be sure of his lineage and for the woman to be good marriage material. Men must be established enough to afford a wife, so we wait until a later age to marry. Women are ready younger."

"Were," she said absently, slowly digesting that piece of information. She had read enough historical novels to understand the facts, but to hear them spoken of as a living reality was completely different.

"Were." He repeated her comment sadly. He reached out and stroked her hand, his thumb resting on her knee. "Tell me about your times. When do you marry?"

"When...." She hesitated, knowing that some things weren't really that different. She cleared her throat. "When we fall in love. Some women marry early, but they usually marry young men. Most of the women I know go to university or college, and then wait a few more years to settle into a career. They marry at around twenty-four or five." She studied his fingers touching hers.

His bronzed brow furrowed as he worked her words around in his head. "This world is very different," he finally said softly.

The recorder clicked off and Hope reached for it, ready to turn over the tape. She pressed Rewind and waited a moment before stopping it in order to check the level of their voices. For a long moment there was nothing, then she heard her own voice. Then nothing. She tried another spot. Then another. The machine hadn't recorded a single word Armand had spoken.

Tears glazed her eyes. She held the small recorder tightly, squeezing it so hard it should have melted from the pressure.

"What is it?" Armand's hands covered hers, prying her fingers loose as he gazed down at the woman he had thought was too strong to cry. "Tell me, please," he said throatily, finally capturing her attention.

"You're a ghost."

Pain flitted across his face. "Yes."

"Really and truly."

"Yes."

"I'm so sorry," she choked out. Her voice sounded as if it came out of a hollow log. Her heart ached with the heaviness of it all. And for the first time, she had to face the depth of her emotional involvement with Armand.

"But you knew this already. Why are you sorry or surprised now?" He reached up to thread her dark hair through his fingers. His touch felt wonderful, but it brought on more tears.

She sniffed, staring at his hand still covering hers. "I knew it, but I didn't believe it. Somehow I really thought, deep down, that it was all a riddle that we would find the answer to, and that you weren't really a ghost at all, just a man like other men."

His fingers touched the bottom of her chin, tilting her face up to his. Her glistening eyes locked with his. "Can I not be both?" he asked softly. "Am I not both now?"

Her bottom lip trembled. "But you're *dead*!" she cried as a tear trickled down her cheek and plopped on his fingers. Her voice held all the disappointment of the child inside her. And, worst of all, she was frightened beyond measure. "I've always been taught that death is when you're supposed to be beyond suffering and so you glide into heaven on angel's wings."

"And for most people, I am sure that is what must happen. For others..." He gave a Gallic shrug, his deep blue eyes as melancholy as hers were, even though he tried to hide behind a smile. "Others must wait for some beautiful young woman to help them find their way."

She swiped at the wet spots on her cheek. Of course he was right, and she had known that all along, but the reality hadn't been brought home until now, when the tape ignored this man who was so flesh-and-blood to her. She *wanted* him to be flesh and blood, but truth had an insidious way of intruding on dreams.

So she was crying for the broken dreams, not the reality, she thought, her eyes widening as she stared up at him. She was crying because she cared too much. . . .

With sure, muscular strength, he circled her waist and pulled her onto his lap, his arms enfolding her securely. He pressed her head close against his chest and crooned words she couldn't understand, but the meaning was clear just the same.

Slowly, very slowly, the tension seeped from her. She raised her hand to cup his jaw, much as he had done to her earlier. "You're very special, Mr. Ghost," she breathed softly.

"So are you, my very modern woman."

"And you're right. You're a man, too. A very firm man."

He grinned ruefully. "With a very real response when a beautiful woman is in my lap, wriggling around to make herself comfortable."

Her smile lighted his eyes, then disappeared slowly with his. "Touch me," Hope said, her whisper as soft as the breeze in the boughs above them.

His eyes never left hers. "Where?" He put his hand on her breast, filling his palm with its softness. "Here?" His fingers drifted along her ribs and belly to rest lightly on the jean-clad apex of her thighs. "Or here?"

Her lids fluttered with each touch, only to open once more, her gaze returning to his face. The openness of her thoughts stirred him further.

Inevitably his lips descended, at last brushing hers when all her breath had fled with the mere anticipation of his kiss. In slow motion he molded his mouth perfectly to hers. He nibbled at her bottom lip, silently seeking entrance. When she opened to him, his tongue danced lightly over her teeth and fenced with her tongue, then began moving in a sensuous rhythm.

Her whole body responded, awash with pleasure that rippled like a shallow stream cascading across a rock bed. Her arms tightened around his neck as she thrust herself closer to the brawn and power of him.

"So sweet," he said raggedly, his lips finally leaving hers. Against the softness of her hair, he whispered, "Touch me. Hold me. Make me feel like a real man again."

And she did. Her hands strayed across his taut muscles, yanking at the shirt tucked tightly into his breeches, then flitting to other parts of him as if to reassure herself that he was really there. Finally the shirt was open, drawn over his head and tossed toward the bed of moss and pine needles nearby. She had been right. His chest was covered with a thick, black mat that curled lovingly around her fingertips.

His hands trembled as he undid the buttons of her blouse, until finally he viewed her soft flesh. "Mmm," he growled against her breast, breathing in her scent as he did. His tongue came out to taste her, lingering until she could no longer stand it.

She unsnapped her jeans, then reached for the buttons of his pants. Suddenly their need for each other seemed to swirl around them like an early-morning mist, isolating them in a world where nothing existed except their touches, their breathing. Their lovemaking.

He entered her just as a slip of wind whistled through the trees, and their sighs matched the sound. Hope felt a fullness, a completeness she had never experienced before, and she wanted to drown in that heavenly sensation.

When he began to move, it seemed as if they had made love a thousand times before. Their hands wandered in synchronicity, caressing bodies and shoulders and arms and legs until all of Hope tingled from his touch.

Her climax came with a shock that shot her eyes open to stare deep into the depths of his and watch the reflection of his own furious need. Then her lids eased shut and she floated back to earth. Furled in his arms and legs, she wanted to stave off reality as long as possible.

"Are you all right?" he asked, brushing aside a stray curl that lay across her cheek.

A smile of utter contentment curled her lips. Her eyelashes were still resting on her cheeks. "Mm-hmm," she sighed.

"Did you enjoy?"

Her smile relaxed into a grin. "Mm-hmm."

"Are you happy?" The note of humor in his voice was obvious. Clearly he would continue asking questions until she gave him more proof.

"Mm-hmm," she sighed again, and puckered her lips to offer a kiss that landed somewhere along the curve of his warm, broad shoulder.

He moved his hips slightly. "Would you care to try again?"

She opened her eyes. Wide. "What?"

His face was a portrait of patience. "I said, would you care to try again?"

"Why?"

"To make perfect what we have just practiced," he said with solemn sincerity. Then she looked into his eyes and saw the devilish laughter lurking there.

"I thought it was perfect."

His brows rose. "Oh? Do you have much to compare it to?"

She knew where he was heading. Still, she was obstinate. "Perfect doesn't need comparisons. It just is."

The silence that followed her statement was filled with other noises. The hauntingly lonely, laughing sound of a loon echoed across the water, and another bird answered. The wind stirred the branches, then stilled. Waves lapped gently at the shore at the bottom of the hill.

"Hope," he began.

"Yes, my ghost?" she whispered against his nipple. She felt it pucker and harden from the caress of her warm breath.

"I would like to try again," he said unsteadily. "Would you?" She raised her head and smiled into his eyes, and he was almost blinded by the sweetness of it.

"Yes. I would." Her hand strayed to the proof of his ardor. "Very much."

And they did.

As the afternoon sun tipped the trees and began to put on a show for them, turning the sky into a palette of pastels, they lay in each other's arms and talked quietly.

He told her of his life on what sounded like an estate near Nice, France. His parents had been wealthy, his father a duke, his older brother a playboy, scattering his favors around the hillsides as if women couldn't wait for him to bestow them. When the wealthy parents of several young girls protested en masse, his brother left, joining a group of other young men headed for the New World to become fur traders.

"And then?"

"Then my father died."

She stroked his side, demonstrating her sympathy. For her the events he described had occurred more than two hundred years ago but for him it was only a few years.

"Father was often ill, but none of us ever realized how ill. One day, he bent over his desk and rested his head on his arms. And he died." He stroked Hope's head, his fingers combing the thick silk of her hair. "It was François's duty to take over as head of the family, but the damn fool was too far away for us to maintain contact with him. At that time France was letting this Northwest Territory slip through her fingers. The British were fighting us, and beginning to win."

He sighed. "Since our family was well-known by the king and his courtiers, they permitted me to come to the Colonies and report on the French and British conflict. In the meantime, I could seek my brother and send him home, where he was needed."

"Did you find him?"

He sighed again. "Yes. As if fate had decreed it, I discovered he was at Fort Charles on the Lac du Bois. I believe you call it the Lake of the Woods. When I reached my brother, he was dressed in buckskins, and he had a bride. She was Ojibwa: young, beautiful and very much in love with him."

"What was her name?"

"Watermark."

She lifted her head to look at him, a question in her eyes. He smiled. "Apparently the name only had meaning for her tribe. No one bothered to relieve my curiosity about it. François did tell me he had married her six months earlier and that she was carrying his child. He was not too pleased to see me because the winter was almost over and he had to continue his work of harvesting pelts. Watermark had to help him."

"You mean he didn't want to go home and become a duke?"

He grinned at her choice of words. "No. He had become too fond of the freedom he found in this wild country ever to be happy maintaining an estate. That would require more work than anything else he had ever done. Even trapping. Also, he knew his wife would not be accepted in France. He had changed too much to go back."

"What about his wife? If she was pregnant, why didn't she stay behind at the fort?"

"Because, alone there, she would be defenseless against the other men. She would not leave his side unless he ordered her to. He would not do that."

"Did you like her, too?"

His eyes crinkled in the corners with the recognition at the true meaning of her question. "I thought she was charming. But, then, I thought all the ladies were charming. But there was only one special lady who caught my attention during my travels. She was standing across the room at the first dance of the season, dressed in a pale green gown and her auburn hair piled atop her head. Her stance informed me she was as royal as a queen, but her brown eyes also told me she was as impudent as a fairy elf."

"Faith."

"You," he said. She stiffened and began to raise herself, but his grip was stronger. Without really struggling, she leaned her head back on his chest as he continued. "I do not know why I am here, or you, but I do know we were here before. You may call it fate, or destiny. Whatever. It does not matter. I know we were together. Our lips might lie, but our souls cannot." His words carried such quiet authority that, for a moment, she believed them. Only for a moment.

"Armand. I like you very much." She crossed her fingers at the understatement. "But I don't believe in fate. I think all this is just a trick of time."

When he shrugged, she felt his muscles tighten and relax from the motion. Delicious. "Believe whatever makes you happy. I know what I know."

"You autocratic, chauvinistic . . ."

His fingers tightened in her hair and turned her mouth to his. "*Oui, ma chérie*, I am all of those. And more," he admitted calmly before claiming her lips once again. Kissing was the only way he knew to keep her from fighting; it was a very effective tactic.

His lips drifted away from hers, and he lay back on the earth. "We will not discuss this again. My beliefs and yours will not mesh before they are ready. Until then, talk is futile."

"My master has spoken," she said dryly.

"That is so," he said, as if she had uttered the truth.

As the early-evening wind cooled off the humid air, Hope fed Armand fried chicken left over from the night before.

"Who is this Colonel Sanders? What war did he fight in?" Armand stared at the picture on the cardboard bucket.

"None that I know of. He's just a Southern gentleman who devised a special blend of spices for his chicken. His title is honorary, bestowed by his friends."

"And he cooks this chicken and then sells it?" He took a big bite out of a drumstick, sinking his white teeth into the meat.

Her stomach tripped as she swallowed her reaction. His virility affected her strongly under normal circumstances; she certainly didn't need to visualize a Tom Jones banquet. "There are probably hundreds of chicken places. Anyway, I think the Colonel died."

"Who continues with his business? His wife?"

She laughed. Armand's imagination was having an impossible time stretching to the boundaries of the country and absorbing the changes since he had last roamed the world. "No, she's gone, too, I'd imagine. But several people formed a company, and now it's a very big business from coast to coast."

His eyes lit up. "So there *is* another coast to this land. I thought there must be."

"Yes, but the so-called Northwest Passage wasn't the way to get there." She reached into one of the bags she had dropped yesterday, pulling out a small atlas. Finding the North American continent, she turned it toward him. "See? Until we built the Panama Canal the only way to the west coast was overland or around the

Horn," she explained, following the trail with her finger.

"This is the land that belongs to America?" he asked, pointing to the United States.

"Yes."

Suddenly she was flooded with questions. And his dismay, as well as his exaltation, were wonderful to watch. "But France has lost all her possessions on this continent! And see the size of Austria! Amazing! Tell me more about this vast land!"

She told him about airplanes and railroads and trucks and cars. She explained the road system. Then she hit upon his favorite topic: food, mentioning other fast-food restaurants that operated around the country. She described French restaurants in New York, and American restaurants in Paris and even in England. He seemed confident and cocky that, of course, the French were the best chefs.

They talked of politics, but because Hope knew only today's status and he knew only yesterday's, their meeting ground was not as secure as with other topics.

They mulled over some of the fashions shown in the magazines, the dreariness of men's clothing, the style and fabric in women's. One common ground was jewelry, abundant in both cultures.

With every topic his eyes became sadder, and Hope's mood matched his. So many years, and so much lost.

"I think I have not enough time to absorb all of the changes in this world," he said, more to himself than to her. Their backs were against the large rock. They stared out at the trees across the lake as the sun melted into pure crayon colors of orange, red, yellow and deep blue. He squinted into the sunset, but she knew that he wasn't seeing it. He was seeing the past. "Help me, Hope. Please, help me to find myself again."

It was the closest he had come to a confession of sadness and frustration. "I will," she said, touching his thigh, aching to wipe away the pain that she knew was just under the surface. "We'll start tonight. Instead of the tape recorder, I'll take notes and then work from there. It will work. I know it." Her tone was so sincere that he had to smile, turning to her with a blinding intensity that drove the breath from her lungs. She cleared her throat. "And in the morning, we'll see if we can find the chest."

"You are a remarkable woman," he said softly.

"Yes, I am, aren't I?" she answered teasingly.

His chin lifted. "Now we will begin."

Hope sighed resignedly. Remarkable she might be, but he was certainly arrogant and self-assured enough for both of them!

THE NEXT MORNING, Hope slept late. She was exhausted from compiling the stack of information about Armand, Faith, and their lives. They had been up half the night when he had decided that he needed another lesson in making love to a very modern woman. It had begun in laughter and ended with the throbbing sweetness of being together. Afterward, she had lain on the sleeping bag and fallen asleep curled around his body, his arms holding her tightly against him.

"It is time to wake up, Hope," Armand said softly. He blew gently in her ear, which made her groan.

"Later."

"No. Now. I have a thousand questions to ask you about your world." His mouth brushed across hers again.

Hope sat up, bending her legs as she tried to focus her gaze on him. He was demanding a history lesson, and all she wanted was sleep. She smiled drearily. That wasn't quite true. She wanted him to make wonderful, tempestuous love to her, as he had last night.

His mouth slowly tilted at the corners. He'd read her mind, and apparently loved the direction her thoughts were taking.

Then she remembered. They were to locate the chest today, if possible. She replied to his unspoken question. "First things first. Let's see if we can begin to unravel the mystery of Armand Santeuil," she said, stifling a yawn.

Eventually they got organized, found a shovel, and began to dig. Armand did the labor, as he had both the muscle and the knowledge of the chest's approximate location.

Hope sat cross-legged on the ground, studying the notes in her lap. The only thing they could do so far was to recover his possessions. The chest was a starting point.

Three hours later she was as frustrated as he was tired. "They must have found it," she declared. "It's the only answer."

Armand wiped his shirtsleeve across his damp forehead and leaned on the shovel. He frowned. "That is not necessarily correct, *ma petite*."

"Of course it is! You've dug a trench all the way around that damn boulder and haven't found it!"

"But what if the underneath of the earth has shifted? Remember, the rock and the oak have changed much since my last visit here. I could be wrong on the exact location. Or perhaps, since this is not my time, I cannot locate it. Perhaps it must be you who finds it?"

Now it was her turn to frown. "I don't know. This isn't earthquake country. But the box itself could have moved, like rocks work their way around and up through cleared and ploughed fields. . . ." she mused. "Could that be possible, I wonder?"

He shrugged. "Anything is possible. We do not seem to be equipped with rules or regulations."

She grinned. "I know. Next time I go to Duluth I'll rent a metal detector," she said, knowing the outfitters in Two Harbors didn't carry anything that wasn't a normal part of a backpacker's equipment. "That should show us the location."

"What is this?"

"It's a machine that locates metal under the earth. Coins, bottle tops, even metal chests."

He nodded. "This is a good tool to have, no?"

"Yes," she said, still smiling. "It is a good tool to have." She glanced at her watch. "In fact, if I hurry, I can make it to Duluth and still be back before dark."

She stood, dusting the seat of her jeans. Armand pitched the shovel up over the lip of the trench. "You are leaving now?"

She nodded. "I might as well. We need to get this show on the road."

"Show?" he asked, vaulting out of the trench.

She chuckled. "Never mind. I'll be back in about three hours. Meanwhile, don't cover the trench. Let's see if this theory of yours holds when I return."

It took her exactly three hours to track down a place that rented metal detectors and then head back. The more she thought of Armand's theory, the more she realized that he could be right.

Suppose she did find the chest and pulled it out, what would happen then? Would he suddenly disappear? She shuddered. Then she would be all alone on the island again, and Armand would probably be with his beloved Faith. . . .

When she returned, the sun was just edging toward the tops of the trees across the lake, marking the needles and leaves with long black shadows.

"I've got it!" she cried as she crested the hill, brandishing the lightweight metal detector in one hand. Armand was standing quietly, contemplating the rock. As she approached, he smiled, but his smile was as sad as her thoughts had been on the road back.

"Hope," he began when she came close to him. His hands rested on her shoulders, kneading them gently. "We do not know what will happen if you find my chest, so I wish to say goodbye to you now. I want you to know that you are very special to me. Very special."

She stared up at him, with tears glistening in her eyes. "Don't say it," she whispered hoarsely, resting her fingers against his lips. "Let's just see what happens, okay? If you go, then you were meant to go now. If you don't . . . Well, we'll see."

He nodded, lightly kissing the tips of her fingers. She forced herself to turn away toward the trench he had dug earlier.

Turning on the machine, she began systematically sweeping over the ground. Within minutes, it was crackling and beeping only inches from the far side of the trench. "Here!" she shouted. "It's got to be the chest!" She set the detector down and started to dig, excitement doubling her strength. The spade hit something hard, and there was a hollow ping. She outlined the object with the shovel. Luck was with them; it was less than two feet down. Even so, it took her another half hour to dislodge the chest from under two hundred years of earth. When she finally brought it up, she was amazed the metal wasn't more corroded.

"That is it," Armand said softly, standing to one side and making no effort to move closer.

Hope's hands trembled as she brushed off the top and sides to get a better look. When new, it must have been a work of great beauty, all brass on brass with now-frayed leather thongs tied around it like ribbon on a present. It was small—about a foot long, and maybe eight or ten inches deep.

She knelt down to study the lock. The keyhole was plugged by over two centuries of soil. It must have required a large key, she mused. The opening was over an inch high. "Get me the screwdriver from the tent, would you?" she asked absently.

"No."

She glanced over her shoulder at him, her brows lifted in surprise. "What do you mean, no?"

"I mean I do not want you to force the lock. The chest is here, and I am still here. Let us think about this before we do something rash. Perhaps if we break the lock, then I will never rest in peace."

Hope leaned back on her heels, her eyes searching his. Did he really feel that way, or was it that he didn't want to leave?

He read her expression perfectly. "Think about this, *ma petite*. When you took the chest out of the ground, nothing happened to me." He looked down at his body. "I am still here. If we break the lock instead of opening it properly, might it not keep me here?"

Her excitement about finding the chest dwindled with the realization that she could have lost him or, worse, could have bound him to earth to roam for eternity. "You're right. I almost forgot why we were doing this." She stared down at the chest that contained his journal and the image of his love. Her curiosity was killing her, but she was also afraid of opening Pandora's box. "We'll wait and see what happens."

He smiled. "We will wait and see," he repeated, relaxing with her decision.

But a part of him wondered if he was willing to wait because he might not get back to wherever he was supposed to be, or because he didn't want to leave Hope....

He wasn't sure.

6

DARKNESS ENFOLDED the hill like a flower whose petals were closing for the night. The Coleman lantern was hooked on a small aspen just feet away from the entrance to the tent. Its flame bled streaks of white gold through the inky blackness, barely touching Hope and Armand with its glow. They sat with their backs to the light, looking down over the cliff side of the hill.

"Are you all right?" Armand was stretched out beside her, his long legs disappearing into the darkness.

She stared out at the shimmering diamonds the moon had scattered upon the water. They had reviewed everything again, trying to determine their next move. The chest sat at the foot of Armand's bedroll, just inside the tent. It was out of their sight, but they both sensed its presence. "I'm fine. Just cold."

"Would you like my sleeping bag?" His voice was soft, but his tone held a teasing quality that in itself warmed her.

She smiled, still staring out at the water. "No, thanks." Her thoughts were consumed by the puzzle pieces that didn't quite fit together.

"So? If you do not care to use my sleeping bag, why do you not come over here and allow me to keep you warm?" he teased.

She turned toward him, a smile of anticipation parting her lips. But then she froze, staring, fear dilating her pupils. "Armand?" she whispered.

He swung his feet around to sit next to her, to comfort her and dispel the fear he read in her eyes. Then he saw what she saw.

He held out a hand, splaying his fingers, and the shadow of the tree could be seen through his palm. *"Mon Dieu,"* he said under his breath, his horrified face a replica of hers.

She reached out as if to stop him from fading, her fingers clamping around his wrist. "Don't go."

Armand held his gaze on her large brown eyes as she looked up pleadingly. His voice was heart-wrenchingly low. "My poor little one. Is this the way it is to end? Am I to find you again only to leave and wander the stars until I find you once more?"

She shook her head. "No!" The denial rasped in her throat as panic flooded through her. She desperately wanted him to stay with her, to be with her.

He smiled sadly. "It would appear that I have no choice in the matter." He held up a hand, staring at it intently as if it belonged to someone else. "The chest must be the answer after all."

She shook her head, denying his words. She needed to tell him so many things, but the words wouldn't come. How could she say that he had made her feel alive again after the degradation of the past months in Central America? He had handed her an exquisite gift: purpose in her life. It was crazy, but she relied on a ghost to give meaning to her life.

Her expression must have told him all, for his fingers brushed her lips with the gentleness of the night breeze. "Do not, little one. Nothing needs to be said."

She kept silent.

"Just stay. Stay with me so I can see you until I cannot see anymore."

She nodded, unshed tears pressuring her eyelids. "I will," she promised huskily. Then she swallowed hard, staring back out at the darkness that had claimed the land. The moon hid behind a bouquet of clouds, and the only light was from the lantern.

"Talk to me," he ordered softly. "Tell me what you are thinking."

"I think that Faith must have been a remarkable young lady. She gave you her love against her father's wishes, which must have been very difficult for her, especially in those times. I also think the voyageurs you spoke of were being manipulated by Faith's father. I'm just not sure how to prove it, or if it's even important."

"And my chest? The men?" His voice was soft and faraway. Fear clawed at her stomach. She couldn't look at him to see what else had happened. Instead she looked at her watch. Midnight. The witching hour. How apropos.

The chest had been found, and without even being opened, it had affected him. What else could happen if they opened it? "I think we need to think this out. I don't know what to do next, but there are several things that come to mind," she finally said. "Tomorrow I'll run into Duluth and check on some old records the library has on people who settled this section of Minnesota. Maybe that will give us a clue."

"How long will you be gone?"

She wanted to tell him that she wouldn't be back at all, couldn't stand to watch him disappear from her life and her island. Instead she said, "Perhaps one night. Or two."

"Then I will wait and try to hold on to my patience," he said in a hollow voice.

"Wait?" She turned to him once more. Her eyes revealed her sorrow. His form and features were still present, but the substance of him was dim.

He nodded. "Wait," he confirmed, giving his familiar shrug. "Where can I go?"

"Wherever you're going now!" she exclaimed, rising to her hands and knees to scuttle closer to him.

"I am going nowhere. I am still here," he said slowly, as if the answer were being whispered in his ear. "I cannot leave yet. I must find the answers before I go."

"Are you crazy?" she screamed, more frustrated than she had ever been before. "You're getting ready to disappear right before my very eyes, and we're *still* pretending there's going to be a tomorrow!"

"Because there will be. Especially for you."

She halted, stunned by his calm words. He was right. Whether he stayed around so she could see him or disappeared so she couldn't, he still wouldn't be at rest. Only she could help him find that rest. Her shoulders slumped, her eyes searching his, only to see infinity.

"Yes," she said quietly, finally understanding what he was saying.

"Faith." He hesitated. "Hope...whatever your name is . . . you were meant to be here for me."

Her sense of identity came back to life for a single, fleeting moment. "No." She shook her head sharply, then stared down, only to look up again. "I'm sup-

posed to be *me*, not Faith. But I don't know anymore.'
She covered her face with her hands, finally allowing
the wave of confusion and remorse to wash over her.

Why was she being tested with this man?

The pretense of sleep wasn't even worth the effort.
They sat quietly, talking the night away. Hope began
spilling out the fears she had experienced in Central
America. "It's really odd," she mused, "but it now
seems as if it all happened to someone else. My health
is back, my energy is back. Even my thoughts don't return to that time. When I first came back here, it was
all I could think of."

"I know that feeling. It is one I have experienced after a battle. But then time heals wounds that you never
believed would be possible to mend."

"Is that what happened between you and Faith, Armand? Has time healed that wound?"

"Perhaps. Or perhaps time found another way to
bridge the gap."

Silence echoed between them, and Hope once more
stared out at the darkness.

"Hope." Armand's voice broke through the silence,
and she turned her head.

"You're returning!" Her eyes widened. He still looked
a bit hazy, but not as much as before.

He smiled. "So it would seem." His voice had re-
gained its wonderful, husky timbre.

She smiled back, all her being concentrated on him.

Her loving expression compelled him to raise his
hand and sift his fingers through her hair. "You are so
beautiful," he murmured.

"So are you," she answered simply. How could she
be coy with a ghost? "Armand? Please hold me.

Just . . . hold me." Suddenly she was frightened by the changes in her thoughts and attitudes, and the need to be comforted was overwhelming.

Muscular arms, more tangible now, enclosed her as he turned her around to sit between his bent legs. Hair-roughened forearms circled her waist, his hands resting just below her breasts. His chin touched the top of her head when he pulled her back against his strong chest. She felt contentment.

Dawn lightened the horizon, tinting the trees black, then brown, then shades of pink. They sat peacefully sharing one of God's miracles.

"You love this country."

"Yes," she said sleepily.

"You love me."

"I don't know you." That was a lie, and she knew it. She covered her mouth as she yawned.

"Yes, you do," he said autocratically. "You love me."

"Don't be so bossy. I'll let you know when I feel love," she murmured grouchily, shifting her weight and snuggling into his now-tangible form. She wriggled her bottom to get closer to him, loving the feel of his lean legs and strong thighs.

His chuckle was low and very, very sexy. "No, you will not, my little one. You will keep it a secret for as long as you can."

She briefly considered arguing, but her lids fluttered closed and she fell asleep, her head against his hard chest.

Armand leaned back against the rough trunk of the tree and closed his eyes. He, too, was sleepy, although he wasn't certain why. Hadn't he been sleeping more than two hundred years?

OUTSIDE THE Duluth post office, Hope stood on the sidewalk checking her mail. The first letter was from her boss.

Joe Bannon's odd scrawl informed her point-blank that she was not to return to work for at least three months, no matter how much of a "stink she put up." Apparently he had handwritten the note so his secretary wouldn't see it, which was thoughtful. There was no sense in letting the world know her boss considered that she wasn't up to par. So much for the good news.

The other letter was from her father, and was as warm as the man could be. He was concerned and thought she needed someone to talk to. He felt responsible for what had happened in Central America. If she wouldn't get "qualified help," perhaps she would be willing to discuss her "problems" with him. It was signed, as usual, Frank.

Problems! Her father didn't know what problems were, until he met a ghost and tried to put him back to rest! Central America was all behind her now. She had more important things to worry about than bad memories.

Hope jammed the letters, along with some bills, into her purse, and began walking toward the main business district, her spirits high. The library was bound to have some answers.

What research she had done before had usually been connected with contemporary politics or a country's history. Such material was kept in separate files and so was easily accessible. But looking for the biographies of people long gone from areas that, at best, had been sparsely populated was new to her. Luckily the local-history section had enough information to get her started. The librarian also told her of the Minnesota Historical Society, an organization that tried to keep records on everyone and anything involved with the state's beginnings. Here she found the caretaker very helpful.

"This should interest you, dear,' the older woman twittered as she sat Hope in front of a screen. "The original ledgers are too brittle to be used, but they're all stored on microfilm. I'll thread this through to start it. You just push this button when you need a copy of whatever you see. It's very simple," she assured Hope, poking her glasses back onto her nose with her index finger.

"What am I looking at?" Hope asked as she scanned the spidery handwriting on the screen in front of her.

"This is the only American copy of the fur-trading records of the fort at Grand Portage that I know of. Grand Portage was first settled in 1660 by men from Duluth, to be used as a trading post for the Indians. These records were sent to businessmen here during the seventeen hundreds. They shouldn't have been, because all records belonged to the North West Fur Company. But mistakes happen, and now we benefit from them."

"Thank you," Hope said, already reading the screen. She refused to admit that the bubble of anticipation sitting in her stomach might not have grounds to be there. She would find something useful. She just knew it.

Six hours later, she finally walked out into the sunshine, her eyes burning. What had she expected? That the puzzle would solve itself by leading her immediately to some miraculous answer? *Yes!* Damn it!

The information was sparse at best. The handwriting was a challenge to read, and almost everything the librarian had dragged out was useless to her quest. The few letters the library had on file had nothing to do with trappers, or the fur business, or even with the French and Indian War. They were personal letters a logger had written to his bride in Boston. Interesting, but not useful.

She *had* found the names of the three men who had killed Armand, though, which was better than nothing. The dates on which they were paid for furs proved they had returned to the fort after killing Armand. She'd also found out that the fort and trading post at Grand Portage was still there, now a national museum.

All day long she had been worried about Armand. Although by dawn he had been completely solid again, she wondered if he would be there when she returned. He might have disappeared completely, this time never to return. After reading the inconclusive information she had found on ghosts, she wasn't sure. A feeling of urgency rushed through her to settle in the pit of her stomach, forcing her steps faster and faster, until she was almost running through the streets. She had to find answers. Fast.

SHE SPENT THE NIGHT in a small hotel on the edge of the city, requesting an early wake-up call. By seven o'clock the next morning she was on her way up the highway, hopefully heading toward the answers she needed.

It was noon by the time she left her car and walked across the parking lot used for the visitors to the Grand Portage Fort and Trading Post. Her hands were clenched at her sides. Armand might once have walked over this very spot. He might have strolled toward that large oak tree with his murderers as they made the deal that would take him overland to see his brother. He might have walked through the wide entrance. . . .

She turned toward the information area. A National Park Service ranger stood behind one of the counters, and her hands itched with the need to touch just a few of the relics displayed in the glass cases.

"May I help you?"

She smiled, excitement glowing in her eyes. "Yes. Can you tell me something about the fort and trading post?"

He handed her a brochure, interest apparent in his glance. "Certainly. There were ten to twelve forts on this location, built between 1660 and 1803. The one you see here now was modeled after the 1803 fort."

Disappointment hit the pit of her stomach like a rock. "It's not the same as the one built in 1762?"

"No, ma'am." He shook his head regretfully.

"Are there any other fort sites up here?" She wasn't going to give up so easily. She couldn't afford to.

"No, ma'am. All the forts were built on top of each other. We're one of the top five richest national sites as far as archeology, but we haven't dug down that far. There's not enough money in the budget—"

Her eyes lit up again. "Records? Are there any records from that time period?"

"Let's see. That was when Duluth set up this post to trade with the Indians. Those records would be in Winnipeg, Paris or London, where they were sent to the North West Fur Company headquarters."

"Do you know how I'd go about getting copies of them?" Hope kept forging ahead. There had to be a way to get more substantial information!

"No, but we have a wonderful library if you'd care to browse. None of the books can be checked out, but you are allowed to make copies."

"But how does anyone do research on this subject?" she finally asked in exasperation. "I'm trying to trace a family that was here. The relatives of a French soldier. Where do I start?"

He shook his head. "As I said, most of that information belongs to Canada or Europe. When the boundary lines were drawn, they got all the good stuff. We just got the land. But then—" he shrugged "—the companies who ran the forts were foreign, so I guess it was only fair."

She couldn't have been more discouraged. She was looking for a needle in a haystack, when all the needles were European-made. "Thank you, anyway," she said, turning toward the section labeled library.

"Wait. There is one more place you could try," he called. Hope turned, her eyes showing doubt. "There's an old man in Duluth, Professor Richards. He used to come up here all the time researching. If I remember right, he's even seen some of the records in London and Paris. He might be able to help you."

She walked slowly toward him, her expression turning from a frown into a smile. "Do you know how to locate him? Would you have his address?"

"I might. Hold on and let me ask one of the gals in the office. She used to help him out with some typing."

Hope tapped her nails impatiently against the counter as she waited for the young ranger to return. It wasn't much, but it was the only lead she had. In fact, it might be her only hope for success, if today was any measure of her sleuthing abilities.

Within five minutes the young man was back, a small slip of notepaper in his hand. "Here it is. Carol says that she still corresponds with him occasionally, and that he'd be the most likely person to help you."

She shook his hand heartily. "Thank you. Thank you so much. I really appreciate this. Thank you." Then she backed out of the room. Smiling widely, she entered the library.

An hour later, notes in hand, Hope practically ran to her car. In Grand Marias she pulled into a small motel and gift shop, bought some paper and envelopes, and wrote a quick note to Professor Richards. Buying a stamp, she mailed the note immediately, praying he would answer his correspondence as soon as he received it.

It was late afternoon when she arrived back at the boat. She started the outboard and moved away from the dock, her eyes restlessly scanning the shore of her island.

The unbearable tension that had gripped her all day slipped away like a silvery fish in deep water. There he was, standing tall and handsome, just where he had been before. She brushed a loose strand of hair away from her face, reveling in the sight of him. Her heart kept on thumping sighs of contentment.

"What happened? Is everything all right?" he asked as she eased the bow onto the shore. He reached down to tie the anchor line to a small tree stump.

"I'm fine," she said breathlessly. Suddenly her blood turned to ice. She'd been so busy getting back to Ar-

mand that she hadn't heard another boat approach.
Armand held out his hand to help her over the side.
"Armand, run!" she urged in a stage whisper as she
turned to see an outboard poke around the next point.
It was one of her neighbors, a man who owned a small
summer cottage on the edge of the lake.

"Don't worry," he said calmly. "He can't see me."

"How do you know?" she whispered out of the side
of her mouth, waving toward her visitor.

Armand kept her hand in his, steadying her as she
placed one foot on shore while the other one was still
in the boat. "Because he couldn't see me earlier this
morning when he came by and I waved." Armand
chuckled.

"Hi there, Mr. Shute. How's the fishing?"

He held up a string of fish. "Just great. Some of the
best trout I've caught in years," he said, frowning at her
a bit and staring at her oddly. "Are you doin' okay, little lady?"

"Who, me? Just fine. Why?" She tried to look surprised, but she was almost unable to answer the old
man. Armand was kissing her wrist, his tongue gently
tracing the path of her veins.

"Just wondering," the older man said. "You look
kinda like one of them garden statues, standing there
like that." His words were a bit garbled by the wad of
tobacco in his cheek.

Her body stiffened, and she slowly swiveled her head
toward Armand. If she had been unable to see him, her
hand would have appeared to be in the air, palm outstretched and curved up like a Balinese dancer's. All her
weight was on the foot on the ground, while the toes of

her other foot were just barely resting on the floor of the boat. Armand was responsible for her balance.

She smiled. "Like it? It's a new yoga position. I'm just practicing." She tried to yank her hand out of his, but Armand, grinning broadly now, would not let go of her.

"Yoga, my dear?" Armand admonished her softly. "Whatever that is, I am hurt. I thought I had caught you in my loving grasp."

"Yoga, eh?" the old man said in a tone akin to awe as he stared at her with his head cocked to one side and watched her hand gyrating erratically in the air. "Well now, ain't that somethin'."

"Yes, yoga," she snapped at Armand. "And it has nothing to do with your grasp." She gave another tug, still trying to wrest her hand out of his.

"My grasp?" the old man repeated, staring down at his hands, then back at her.

"Yes. No!" She jerked her hand again. "I mean, it's just a new position."

"Well, okay then." Mr. Shute turned away, revving his motor. "If you need any help, jest holler," he shouted over his shoulder, obviously convinced that she was a bit tetched in the head.

Hope watched him carefully turn his boat around and head for his own small cove, knowing she had probably just made a fool of herself. No "probably" about it. She *had* made a fool of herself.

"How much of this yoga do you think he knows?" Armand asked softly, laughter tingeing his voice.

"Not much, I hope," she answered testily, ready to turn on him for his part in the farce that had just been performed.

Armand's brows lifted quizzically. "But he offered to help you with it."

That did it. She laughed. She laughed so hard that she fell into his arms, and tears flooded her cheeks. Slowly they sank to the ground, holding each other as all the tensions of the past week ebbed away. The feelings of contentment that flowed between them were almost visible.

They finally got to their feet and started up the hill. Every few steps Armand would glance over his shoulder at her, his dark eyes sending messages that felt like electrical currents running down her back.

By the time they reached the hilltop, the sun had begun its late-afternoon crayon coloring of their world. Armand held her in his arms as she leaned her head against the strength of his chest. "It is time for you to go home and get into bed," he said softly, kissing the top of her head. "You need a hot bath and a good night's rest after all your work. We will talk in the morning, my Hope."

"Mm-hmm," she murmured, too tired even to form words.

"So, go," he ordered, taking her by the shoulders and pointing her toward the farmhouse. "I will walk you half the way."

"Only half?" she teased.

"That is as far as I can go," he reminded her gently, and her smile disappeared.

When they reached the spot where the small pine tree grew, Armand stopped. "Good night, my sweet." He brushed his lips lightly against hers.

"Good night," she said softly, wishing she could remain in his arms all night, yet knowing she needed sleep and a bath, not necessarily in that order.

She plodded slowly toward the house. In minutes she was undressed, bathed and in bed. But her eyes kept popping open to search the heavens outside her window for answers that weren't there. Morning arrived slowly.

Throwing on some jeans and a loose-knit emerald sweater, Hope brushed her teeth and washed her face without bothering to look in the mirror. She brushed her long hair and clipped it back with a barrette, then pushed her feet into dark tan deck shoes.

She heated two frozen breakfasts and together with her notes from the day before, carried them carefully up the hill. When she reached the closed tent flap, she set everything down on the grass.

"Wake up, sleepyhead. The sun's been up for hours! Besides, you have to eat, and then we have to talk." She pushed aside the flap and reached around the small chest to grab the corner of the sleeping bag. It was empty.

Her hand froze in midair and her heart thumped heavily against her breast. He was gone. He had faded away again during the night and somehow hadn't returned.

She dropped heavily to the ground, her hand still clutching the edge of the sleeping bag. She closed her eyes against the pain that invaded her.

Birds whistled cheery songs to each other. A fish or two splashed in the lake. An old French tune drifted through the air, faint at first, but growing stronger with each bar.

Hope lifted her head, straining to hear better. The sound came closer. She stood up, motionless as she tried to discern its source. Her heart pumped faster. No one else knew that song. Not even Faith. Armand had told her so.

Slowly she turned. Her fingers dug into the sturdy fabric of her jeans. When at last his dark head bobbed above the side of the hill, joy enveloped her, and she dashed toward the path he was following.

"You're here!" she cried as he halted in front of her, a makeshift fishing pole in one hand.

"Where else was I supposed to be, hmm?" he asked indulgently, one brow raised.

"Gone."

His smile faded. He leaned his pole against a tree trunk and reached for her, gently gathering her in his arms. His lips teased the side of her neck, and he breathed in her scent before releasing a contented sigh. His arms tightened around her. "No. I did not go away," he said huskily, pulling back slightly to look into her eyes. "I am very strong in the morning, my sweet."

She offered him a shaky smile. "That's what they all say." Unable to stay her hand, she touched the side of his jaw, then traced the corded muscle down the side of his neck and onto his broad shoulder. Her fingertips paused on the pulse point at his throat.

His eyes smoldered like cinders. He drew her back into his embrace, leaning the full weight of her body against his, running his hands over the curve of her hips and waist, stopping only when he reached the pert thrust of her unbound breasts. "I am still astonished that ladies are allowed to wear so few clothes. Pleased . . . but astonished."

"But you only have on a shirt and a pair of pants. No underwear." Her amused eyes told him how much she had loved that discovery, and he grinned at her wolfishly.

"Some men search the world over to find someone like you, my Hope. A woman who knows her own body well and enjoys what happiness it brings both to her and her lover."

"Most of those men you describe were probably way ahead of their time. Women always liked what men did, but were told that they shouldn't let anyone know for fear of being labeled hussies," she explained, rocking gently against his pelvis.

"My mother never enjoyed it," he said autocratically.

"Poor mother," she whispered, kissing his throat and tasting the salty tang of his skin.

"She was a lady, through and through. A duchess who knew that everything must be done just so, and who did it with panache."

"You mean her days were filled with work, and her nights were without joy. How terribly sad." Her hands stroked his shoulders from neck to biceps, then back again.

His eyes were becoming heavy-lidded with desire. "But that life was right for her," he insisted. "My father's mistress served him very well."

"Poor father," she murmured consolingly, nibbling on the strong column of his throat. "It's a good thing he wasn't born in this time, or he would have been kicked out by his good wife. Besides, if one wants something, isn't it better to have it next to you in bed, rather than to have to get dressed to go out and then undressed to make love, then dressed once more to get back home? How bothersome."

"I will have to think about that. I think you have turned logic inside out."

He kissed the tip of her nose, then her forehead and her cheeks, and she couldn't even chuckle at the thought of disarming him. She couldn't think, period.

"Kiss me here," she ordered before taking his head in her hands and placing his mouth over hers where it belonged.

Long moments later she reluctantly moved out of his arms and went back to the tent to retrieve the breakfast trays. "Here. I'd better feed you before you fade away from lack of nutrition. Then I want to tell you what I've found out."

Reluctantly, he accepted the tray. Peeping under the tinfoil, he asked, "What is it?"

"French toast and sausage," she explained, reclasping her barrette around the thick cord of shiny dark hair at her neck.

"French toast? Impossible." He shook his head as he stared at the concoction he held. "This is something invented by the English, I am sure. We French would never call this by our national name," he said, curling his lip in what she was sure was supposed to be utter disdain.

Unimpressed, she laughed. "Eat it. You'll love it."

"I hope what you found is better than this looks," he said, still eyeing the tin plate of food. But his face held a trace of a smile as he sat down. Leaning against the tree trunk, he tasted his breakfast.

His smile became a frown of consternation. Certainly Hope was making a joke when she called this

French toast, he thought. The French never joked about food, and this tasted like a sickeningly sweet sponge.

Hope ate slowly, her mind occupied with her finds, wondering if Armand would be angry when he learned that his enemies had succeeded. They had done very well for themselves, if the ledger pages were correct, and she was sure they were. She knew she'd feel bitter if she were in his place....

Grabbing up the research papers, she sat in front of him and gathered her thoughts. But she made the mistake of looking at him, and she was suffused with a sense of wonder. He was so real, so very wonderful.... She shook her head to break the mood. "We need to talk." Her voice sounded breathless.

His dark brows lifted. "Please do so," he said as he reached for her hand once more. "I have been waiting all my life for a woman who talks as little as you do," he teased. "But now that I have found you, I would like to hear your voice a little more often."

"Don't be complacent," she laughed. "You may disappear yet."

His smile waned. "I hope not yet. There are so many things I want to say to you. Do with you."

Her hand traced the line of his cheek. She loved his lean, strong face. It was a face one could count on. Dream about. "I know. I didn't mean that. You're still here, so I think you'll stay a while."

He shook his head. "Let us not delude ourselves. I will go someday. I may not want to, I may not be ready. But I will disappear. I have come to terms with that over the past few days."

"You have?" Her eyes searched his. "Why haven't I?" she murmured, as if to herself.

"Perhaps because this is your time to live, not to come to terms with death." He twisted his head and kissed her caressing palm. "I am here only to have you help me. When you go . . ." He let the rest of the sentence drift away, but she knew what he meant. When winter came, she would have to leave or be stranded. And when she left, he would be alone.

Crossing her arms, she stared at the blue water. She could feel Armand behind her, waiting calmly for her to speak. Finally she faced him. "I found some records—ledgers from a merchant in Duluth who was dealing with Grand Portage during the middle seventeen-hundreds."

He raised his brows. "And?"

"One of the men, François Tourbet, apparently married an Indian girl. They worked together selling furs in Grand Portage. It seems he died a few years later, and his account was settled on his wife and child. Henri Houdon stayed at Grand Portage instead of trapping. I don't know where he got the money, because he wasn't paid by the post, except once, although he did buy supplies."

"Go on," he said, staring out at the blue water below the jutting cliff.

"The third man—" she glanced quickly at the sheets in her hand "—Jacques Pillon, made a small fortune if the records are correct. The records show constant amounts of money given to him in payment for furs, yet he was never gone from the fort for very long. All the accounts are only three or four weeks apart."

"What else?"

She sighed. "I went to Grand Portage. It seems that there are no other records concerning Grand Portage left in the United States. If I need more information, I'll have to go to the museums, or the offices of the Hudson's Bay Company or the North West Fur Company. In Europe."

'No." It was said softly, but with stubborn conviction. "You will not travel that far. There has to be another answer."

"There are a few more sources to check out. But most of the records in Minnesota have to do with the logging industry, not fur-trading." She looked at him. "But I do have an excellent lead. There's a historian who is fascinated with the French occupation. He's writing a book on the Northern Arrowhead families. He might have something we can use."

"The French ownership," Armand corrected. "Was it taken from us? By whom? New France was becoming more British every day. Even the Scots were claiming our land."

"Everything France owned in the Northwest Territory was signed over to the British in 1763, one year after you were here."

"Very well," he said, as if the point were not important enough to argue about.

"Anyway, I'll be going back to Duluth in four or five days, and I'll see if I can get ahold of the historian. He might know more about what happened to the men who killed you."

Armand began to pace, his boots scuffing through leaves and pine needles along the bluff. "Then we shall know soon." He halted his restless march, staring at her as a new concept occurred to him. "Is there any mention of the key? The one that opens the chest?"

She shook her head. "No, not yet." She'd been afraid he would ask that question. How did one go about finding a two-hundred-year-old lost key? It was impossible...

"You will find it," he said with a certainty that nettled her.

"How do you know?" she demanded. "After more than two hundred years, it could well be lost! The United States is big enough to hide thousands of people a year, let alone one small ivory key that's older than the country!"

"The country has always been here," he admonished as if speaking to a child.

"I mean the Declaration of Independence. It wasn't signed until 1776!"

"Really? You must tell me about this declaration sometime. I do not remember you mentioning it before."

She grinned reluctantly. "Do you think you're going to divert me from an honest tantrum by changing the subject?"

"I do not know, *chérie*. But it was worth the attempt." His blue eyes twinkled. "However, if that diversion does not work, I have another in mind. One that would be much more pleasant for both of us."

Against her will, he had her laughing again. "You're incorrigible!" she exclaimed, allowing herself to be enveloped in his arms once more.

"What is this incorrigible?" he murmured, his lips tasting the side of her throat. "Is it a compliment? Does it mean that I am in love with you, or that you melt when I touch you? Stroke the core of you? Taste of you?"

Her arms circled his neck. "No," she drawled, a twinkle in her eyes. "It means that you're brazen, egotistical and spoiled rotten, and there is no hope for redemption. No wonder women fell at your feet."

"Alas, no, *chérie*," he murmured. "Into my arms, but never at my feet, much to my dismay."

Before she could retaliate, his lips had covered hers with a kiss that sent all thoughts scurrying away like mice escaping a hungry cat.

She knew her information had upset him. She could see it in his eyes. Three men who had obviously been involved in killing him went on to succeed in their lives without retribution. But if he wanted to forget in an embrace, the least she could do was help him.

Her arms tightened as she allowed him to assume the mastery of their lovemaking. After all, he was French. Surely she should allow a Frenchman to do what he does best . . .

7

SHE HAD BEEN RIGHT—Armand was upset by the news she had delivered. Thinking she had dozed off, he'd crept from her side and gone for a walk. She glanced at the small black watch on her wrist. A long walk, apparently; he'd been gone almost three hours. It was after noon, and the sun was at its warmest. She knew that if she looked she'd probably find him down at the cliff, skipping stones or just staring into the water.

Damn it! Didn't he know that she needed to comfort him? And comfort herself, as well . . .

She loved Armand, and she wanted to be with him for as long a time as he had left. She didn't know how or when she had fallen in love, but there certainly hadn't been any brilliant light that flooded her with truth and knowledge. Instead, love had seeped slowly into the very core of her being, growing from a seedling to an oak, until it filled every corner of her mind and body. It was something she just *knew*, and now she could not deny it to herself.

Imagine being in love with a man who was a chauvinist before Chauvin! A smile tipped up the corners of her mouth. Armand was born to lord it over women—all women. It was his nature. But it was also a sign of the times—his times.

There was something good about his attitude, though. At first she couldn't quite put her finger on it.

But then it came. He was strong. And that strength gave her a feeling of sweet security she had never felt with any other man. He was protective without being possessive. Strong without being overpowering. He could speak in the softest of whispers, yet project great authority.

The sound of crackling leaves brought her head up. Her gaze darted among the trees, only to lock onto the startling blue eyes of the man who filled her thoughts. Neither she nor Armand moved.

Little by little, every muscle in her body became taut. His expression was more eloquent than any words could have been, telling her that they were meant to be together for whatever time was left.

Her eyes spoke volumes, too, telling him she needed him close to her. Expressing feelings she was only just beginning to grasp.

She watched him as he walked toward her with a grace that was part animal and part man. His every muscle and bone worked together to create a masterpiece of motion that almost took her breath away.

Armand sank to the ground across from her. He cleared his throat then reached out, his fingers lingering to limn the outline of her ear. "Are you so uncertain, my Hope?"

"Yes."

"Of me, or yourself?"

She looked up. "Both."

"And do you not believe that I could be unsure also?" Sadness touched his eyes, revealing a deep vulnerability that almost shocked her. "I am the one who must knock down stone walls to get to the heart of you, my love. Every time I make an advance to get closer, you fight me, because you believe, no matter what I tell you, that you are only a replacement for another. By now, we both should know that this is not true. A reminder, yes. A replacement, no." His tone was so melancholy that it oozed over her like warm syrup. He was telling her of his love for her, not for another woman!

Her voice was barely a whisper. "Are you sure?"

"Yes." She heard no doubt in his voice, and she searched his face, seeking any flaw in his conviction. There was none.

"I love you," she said quietly, gaining strength from the sound of the words themselves. Once they were said, released into the warm summer breeze, a weight lifted from her body and she felt as light and trembly as the aspen leaves shimmering overhead. "And because I love you, I'm scared, Armand."

His eyes glowed. "I know. I have been waiting for you to admit it."

Her hand rose to cradle his hand against her face. "Whether time or the gods worked against us as a joke, or brought us together for some purpose, I do not care, Hope. I have you now. That is all that matters."

She was almost afraid to say the words, but she had no choice. "And when you go?"

He shrugged fatalistically. He wanted to hold her, crush her to him so they could blend together and never be separated. But that was not to be, and he knew it. "I will simply go. It is out of our hands. But during the time I am here, I want to be with you. To love you. To try to take care of you."

It was her turn to smile. "Even if I'm stubborn and mean?"

Discover deliciously different romance with 4 Free Novels from

Harlequin Temptation ™

Sit back and enjoy four exciting romances—yours **FREE** from Harlequin Reader Service! But wait . . . there's *even more* to this great offer!

HARLEQUIN FOLDING UMBRELLA— ABSOLUTELY FREE! You'll love your Harlequin umbrella. Its bright color will cheer you up on even the gloomiest day. It's made of rugged nylon to last for years and is so compact (folds to 15") you can carry it in your purse or briefcase. This folding umbrella is yours free with this offer!

PLUS A FREE MYSTERY GIFT—a surprise bonus that will delight you!

All this just for trying our Reader Service!

MONEY-SAVING HOME DELIVERY!

Once you receive your 4 FREE books and gifts, you'll be able to preview more great romance reading in the convenience of your own home at less than retail prices. Every month we'll deliver 4 brand-new Harlequin Temptation novels right to your door months before they appear in stores. If you decide to keep them, they'll be yours for only $2.24 each! That's .26¢ less per book than what you pay in stores—with no additional charges for home delivery.

SPECIAL EXTRAS—FREE!

You'll also get our newsletter with each shipment, packed with news of your favorite authors and upcoming books— FREE! And as a valued reader, we'll be sending you additional free gifts from time to time—as a token of our appreciation.

BE TEMPTED! COMPLETE, DETACH AND MAIL YOUR POSTPAID ORDER CARD TODAY AND RECEIVE 4 FREE BOOKS, A FOLDING UMBRELLA AND MYSTERY GIFT—PLUS LOTS MORE!

A FREE
Folding Umbrella

and Mystery Gift *await you, too!*

Harlequin Temptation™

Harlequin Reader Service®
901 Fuhrmann Blvd., P.O. Box 1394, Buffalo, NY 14240-9963

☐ **YES!** Please rush me my four Harlequin Temptation novels with my FREE Folding Umbrella and Mystery Gift. As explained on the opposite page, I understand that I am under no obligation to purchase any books. The free books and gifts remain mine to keep.

142 CIX MDMZ

NAME _____
(please print)

ADDRESS _____ APT. _____

CITY _____ STATE _____ ZIP CODE _____

Offer limited to one per household and not valid for present subscribers. Prices subject to change.

PRINTED IN U.S.A.

HARLEQUIN READER SERVICE "NO-RISK" GUARANTEE

- There's no obligation to buy—and the free books and gifts remain yours to keep.
- You pay the lowest price possible and receive books before they appear in stores.
- You may end your subscription anytime—just write and let us know.

BUSINESS REPLY CARD

First Class   Permit No. 717   Buffalo, NY

Postage will be paid by addressee

Harlequin Reader Service
901 Fuhrmann Blvd.
P.O. Box 1394
Buffalo, NY 14240-9963

NO POSTAGE
NECESSARY
IF MAILED
IN THE
UNITED STATES

He nodded. "Yes, even when you withdraw from me in anger and frustration. Most especially then. Your soul is mine, Hope, just as mine is yours."

Tears flooded her eyes as she became aware of the depth of his commitment.

"When you cry, I will wipe your tears away. When you laugh, I will laugh with you. When you misbehave, I will punish you." His hand drifted to her shoulder, then dropped lightly to the bare skin just above the fullness of her breast. "When you love, it will be only with me."

The tears stopped. "Punish?"

"Punish. Every woman needs a beating now and again."

"Not on your life."

He grinned. "Ah, but my Hope, you have no idea how wonderful a beating can be."

Her look became indignant. "I want to keep it that way, too, Armand. It might have been done in your time, but in my time women don't stand for it."

He smiled as her meaning became clear. "I will never be hurtful."

"Then you will never punish."

"And you will never misbehave."

They smiled at the same time, realizing how ridiculous their conversation had become. Then came another realization: they were bound together by some powerful connection that let them share their thoughts. Even their hearts.

"You seem very content," he murmured, kissing the auburn hair on top of her head as his sun-browned hands played games across the softness of her back.

"Only because I am, and you know it." She chuckled softly.

"Good." His voice was laced with satisfaction.

"Conceited."

"Yes. And it is well deserved."

She chuckled again, only this time she raised her head to look into twinkling eyes. "Every inch the Frenchman."

"What else could I possibly be, *chérie*?"

Laughing, she touched his mouth with hers, then sat up, pushing her hair away from her face. She reveled in the touch of the sun spiking through the trees to bathe them both in soft green light that seemed almost magical. They still touched, were still connected, and it felt so very, very right. "Nothing else. For you it would be impossible to be anything but the French aristocrat. You fit the part all too well."

His hands began to explore her waist appreciatively, his blue eyes memorizing the path his hands were following. They examined the flatness of her stomach, then wandered slowly up to cup her breasts. "Does that please you?"

Her laughter dissolved. "Yes. Oh, yes," she said solemnly, as if making a vow. "You please me so much it frightens me."

She felt her heart tearing into a thousand different pieces. Her eyes closed as she sought to block out the pain that looking at him represented now. But it didn't work. The pain—myriad blades stabbing into her midsection—was agony. She opened her eyes again and bent over him, touching her lips to his in silent supplication.

FOR THE NEXT WEEK they didn't discuss the problem of solving his murder, as if the subject were taboo. Hope was frustrated by her inability to work on the mystery, but there was nothing she could do except to give Professor Richards time to answer her letter.. That fact made it easier to relax and enjoy Armand's company without feeling guilty.

Nevertheless, thoughts lingered in the recesses of her mind, haunting her at odd moments, day and night. The old, tarnished brass chest at the foot of his sleeping bag was a constant reminder. Occasionally, she could see shadows cross his face, and she knew he had the same thoughts.

She lived with him in the tent at the top of the hill, always falling asleep before he began his "disappearing act." She knew that it was cowardly, and that it was a form of denial. Her heart yearned for him to stay with her, to love her, but her mind was too wise to believe he would.

AT THE END of the week, Hope finally broached the subject they had both been avoiding. As she spoke, she stared at the ground where a picnic lunch was spread. "I should have an answer from the professor I told you about. The one who's studying the history of the families in this area. He might have a lead." She bit into a sandwich as if to force the words back down her throat.

He sighed with relief. At last she was discussing it. He examined his sandwich with a jaundiced eye. The bread was a dark rye with little seeds on it, and he wasn't at all sure it was healthy. Didn't anyone make good French bread, or was this supposed to be a substitute of some sort? He bit into it, wishing there were more foods he recognized.

As her silence continued, his brows raised. "When?" he asked around the gluey concoction that insisted on cementing his tongue to the roof of his mouth.

"At the end of the week."

"And?"

"And nothing!" she snapped. "I just thought I'd inform you that I'm leaving, just in case you should miss me and wonder where I was."

He swallowed, then set the sandwich carefully on its wrapper. It should have been fed to the English in times of war. They would never have been able to issue orders with such a concoction in their mouths. "I will miss you, Hope, but not this food," he said disgustedly, knowing that would distract her. Besides, it was true.

She couldn't help her grin. "It was invented by an English lord, the Earl of Sandwich. I understand he was a rake and a gambler. Inventing the sandwich was the only good thing he ever did." Armand's expression challenged her last statement, but he didn't reply. "I'll also do some grocery shopping," she promised.

His answering look conveyed disbelief that the menu would improve over what she had been feeding him. Her grin dissolved into a giggle.

Reluctantly, he began laughing, too, the delightful sound tugging at Hope's heart. "Do you think you might find a small steak of beef and some potatoes? Perhaps some beans? A mushroom or two? One perfect onion?"

"Perhaps," she replied teasingly.

"How long will you be gone?"

"About two or three days. I need to gather all the clues I can, and I also have to look through some newspapers from the late eighteen hundreds for any articles on Minnesota before it was a state."

He ran his fingers through his hair, his brow furrowed. "I did not realize it would be so long."

She reached over to touch his thigh, her hand resting there gently. "But it's necessary. This way I won't have to make so many trips. I'll be back as soon as I can," she promised.

"I know."

Reality once again infiltrated their intimacy, to chill the very air around them. Hope sought desperately to dispel it, but she didn't know how. "Armand, talk to me. About anything. Please."

"All right, *chérie*," he said calmly, wrapping the rest of his sandwich in waxed paper. "I shall tell you of my first days at court."

"At the king's court?"

His surprise was evident. "But of course. Where else is there a court?"

Hope smiled. "But of course. Go on," she urged.

Before he began, Armand leaned back, propping himself against the fat tree trunk behind him, and Hope rested against him. He wrapped his arms around her waist. "Now, where was I?"

"In court. How old were you?"

"I had just reached my manhood, about thirteen, I should think."

"Manhood?" She twisted her neck to stare at him. "How did you know? Or is it a ceremony?"

His chest moved with his chuckle, vibrating through her back and quickening her heartbeat. "There was no ceremony, my sweet. It was just a statement of fact. I was then old enough to make babies."

This time she understood, but played the innocent anyway. "But how did you know? Had you tried?"

His arms tightened around her waist. "That, my love, is none of your business. I knew. That was sufficient."

Hope gave a mock sigh. "Okay, continue."

He kissed the top of her head as consolation for his refusal to elaborate. "My father decided that my brother and I—François was fifteen and pretended to be very much older then—should see Versailles and begin to appreciate what being a member of the French nobility meant."

"Sounds like a true Frenchman," Hope interjected sarcastically, not admitting how impressed she was with the palace itself. She had been there several years ago and knew of the golden splendor he had experienced so personally.

Her comment flew right over his head. "Of course. We rode in my father's carriage, and the journey took four days from our estate. By the time we finally reached the road to the entrance of Versailles, both my brother and I had given up any pretense of being grown-up and blasé. The palace was a glittering masterpiece of white and gold blazing in the sun, just as our king did, with a heavenly light. There were people everywhere: nobles, merchants, servants, soldiers, peasants, and the most beautiful women I had ever seen in my life. Over three thousand subjects lived there. It was a city unto itself."

He stopped. Hope opened her eyes and twisted around to stare at him again. "Go on. What else?" she asked quietly, almost afraid to intrude upon his thoughts. But her mind had already conjured up the scene he had described, and she wanted to visualize the rest.

He looked down at her for a moment, but it was as if he was seeing something, or someone, else. Then he smiled. "Our coach went through the huge black iron gates tipped with gold and stopped at a porte cochere, one of the many entrances. There, Papa gave us our final reminders on courtly behavior, which we promptly forgot. François and I poured out of the coach, looking for all the world like two overgrown pups. At that moment, I raised my head and stared down the covered hallway leading to the interior of the palace. My breath was taken away at my first glimpse of the most beautiful woman I had ever seen coming down the hallway toward us."

"Who was she?" Hope's voice was barely a whisper. She could feel his shrug as he continued.

"Just one of the many courtesans who made up the court. She was about seventeen or so, whose sole purpose was to give the noblemen of the court a sweet andfjheavenly time. Her family estate had been confiscated when her father was sent to the Bastille. She had the choice of living as she did or finding herself alone, begging on the streets of Paris." His voice changed, taking on a slight edge. "She made her choice, this clever woman, to occupy beds that were warmer and softer than the filthy cobblestone streets."

"Did you fall in love with her?"

"For a little while," he answered. A rock dropped into the pit of Hope's stomach. "I must have followed her around for days, begging for favors—a look, a smile, a pat on the head. I am sure I much resembled an overly tall fawning lapdog. Even in those days I was taller than most of my peers. My mother used to say I was a throwback to a German princess my great-grandfather married. I understand she was so tall that the top of his head came only to her breast." An indolent smile brushed his lips as he remembered himself in those days, all arms and legs and eagerness.

"What happened?"

"The usual thing. After a week of my pestering her, she took me to her bed and taught me what being a man was all about." His voice was so matter-of-fact, so normal, that she felt instant rage that he should be so cavalier about his experience.

"And was it everything you'd expected it to be?" She bit off each word.

His arms tightened around her as he chuckled. "At that age, *ma chérie,* anything is heaven! Yes, it was more than I had dreamed, and then some. But, looking back, I am sure the best part was that my brother never shared Marie's bed. He had to settle for someone else."

Hope swallowed hard to ease the lump in her throat. "And did you miss her after you left?"

"I am sure I did, but I had so much delightful, newfound knowledge that I was anxious to return home and try it out on some other maidens. Marie was merely the person who first taught me the wonders of lovemaking, not the first one to teach me to love."

"I see." Her voice was a bare whisper, her jealousy blotting out everything else.

"I do not think you do, *ma chérie.* Marie was at Versailles for that one reason. Surely there are women around today who serve the same purpose, are there not?"

"Yes. But I don't know them, or anyone else who does," she finally admitted.

"Because no one speaks of using such women, does that mean that they do not exist, or that they do not serve the young men of today?"

"No."

"Then forgive me my transgressions, Hope," he said as he smoothed her hair, his voice soft and sincere. "I was a boy, and I needed guidance in pleasing women. She was my teacher. It was all over the day our carriage left the courtyard on our journey home." He kissed her temple, his breath warm against her skin. "However, that was not the story I was about to tell you. I was going to describe the treasures of the Versailles—the paintings and furnishings, not the woman and intrigues. There was one painting there that I will never forget. It was a portrait of a young woman with a mysterious smile. Someday I will describe it to you..."

"Another time," she murmured, pretending sleepiness. She had seen the Mona Lisa.

"Another time," he repeated, sighing. There was no need for memories when Hope was in his arms.

Silently they lay there together, each caught up in their own thoughts. The sun slowly began its descent and fired the sky with pastel beauty.

They were poles apart on so many things, Hope mused. His story should have been just one more example of how mismatched they were. But when he held her like this and she could smell the sensual, musky scent of him, feel the tight muscles of his legs next to hers, his touch on her arms and breasts, she didn't think about his Versailles having existed more than two hundred years ago. Those sensations were here—now.

Before allowing her eyes to droop shut, she wondered briefly why his erotic tale had made him seem even more real to her. A ghost telling about a life that had taken place hundreds of years ago should have made the gap between them wider.

Her last thought was that people hadn't really changed over the years. They were still the same...

ARMAND STOOD on the crest of the hill and watched Hope's small boat head toward the other end of the lake, aimed toward what Hope called an automobile. He picked up the double spyglass she called binoculars and focused them on the swift craft, his eyes scanning her face carefully for confirmation that she would return.

The gurgle of the boat's motor echoed eerily across the lake. His hands clenched the glasses tighter as his Hope grew smaller in the distance. He closed his eyes a moment, letting the glasses hang by the strap around his neck.

Hope. Hope was everything to him. She was more than his *femme*, his love, his confidante. She was as sweet as a wildflower and as prickly as a briar patch. She was his *églantier*, his own sweetbriar. He felt as if she were the other half of his soul. She was Faith—all grown up.

Yes, he had loved Faith, but in many ways it was a protective kind of love. He would have sheltered her from the world and its sorrows, because she had not been strong enough or competent enough to endure the realities of pain and hardship. Though he had known that, he had pressed her to make a decision, to marry him or stay with her father.

He had never known what her choice had been. But he had had niggling doubts about her being at their arranged meeting place the night they were to leave. The truth was that he hadn't trusted her loyalty to him enough to assure himself that she would choose him over her father.

If her mother had allowed her to grow up, instead of coddling her like a little porcelain doll . . . If her father had treated her more as a woman than a commodity, or a property to be sold to the highest bidder, it might have been different.

But now it was Hope who consumed his thoughts. She took care of him, protected him, kept him safe and well. She had taken the lead because he could not. Confined to a shelf of an island that barely allowed him access to four feet of water, he had been the one who needed sheltering, not Hope.

He wanted to rail against the gods for doing this to him, to scream at the elements for forcing him to live past his time, never to find the peaceful rest others had. Yet he wanted to thank the same gods for giving him this opportunity to love a woman as worthy as Hope.

His lips moved in silent prayer. If he had only one wish, it would be that the gods be generous and give him one more chance, so that he could spend whatever they deemed to be his life with Hope. Hope had become his *douceur de vivre*, his sweetness of life. She was more his life and love than he had ever dreamed possible.

Faith had been his first chance for happiness; Hope his second chance. *Mon Dieu*, but he needed one more so that he could live a normal, loving life with the woman who meant everything to him. A third chance . . .

HOPE OFFERED UP A PRAYER to the bright blue sky. She stood at the entrance to the post office and opened the letter from Professor Richards; it had been delivered to her box that morning. Immediately, she found a telephone and a quarter, and dialed the professor's number. It took a little more than a minute to make an appointment to see him. All the way to his house, Hope told herself to calm down and not to pin all her hopes on his research. But that was practically impossible.

Professor Richards was a delightful example of an absentminded professor, but sharp brown eyes peeked out over his bifocals. In his late sixties, he was thin to the point of gauntness, and his slightly stooped shoulders made him look as if he had been hunched over a desk all his life.

"These men were here for quite a while, then, according to the fur records?" he asked over the piles of papers on his desk.

Seated across from him, Hope leaned forward eagerly. "Yes," she said, handing him the names and copies of the fur-trader's ledgers she had picked up at the library. "I've already consulted these sources."

He glanced at the papers, then put them to one side. "I'll see what I can do, my dear. I have copies of some family records that might help. You know, private letters, bibles. They're undocumented, of course, as far as historical accuracy goes, but then most things were in those times." He leaned back and rubbed the bridge of his nose. "Most people kept journals or sent letters, but more often than not, they exaggerated more than the best of fishermen." He wrung a smile from her before continuing. "But if I have the names, I'm sure to run across information of some kind."

"Thank you, Professor Richards. I'd appreciate anything you can find." She stood and held out her hand. "I'm staying at the hotel in the east end of town. The telephone number is on the corner of that paper."

He unfolded himself out of his chair and offered her an absent handshake. Obviously his mind had already drifted somewhere else. "Goodbye, my dear. I'll give you a call if I find anything," he said before sitting down and shuffling through his papers once again.

Hope was heading toward the door when his voice stopped her.

"Oh, Miss Langston? I see here that one of the names is Captain Trevor."

"Yes?" She held her breath, waiting impatiently for the old gentleman to continue. When he didn't say anything more, she prompted him. "He used to be at Port Huron in Michigan. He had a daughter named Faith."

The professor took off his glasses and wiped them on a large handkerchief. "Hmm, yes. I'm sure it's the same one, then."

"The same one as what?"

"Do you know the Haddington Family? Lovely family, all of them. And so devoted to keeping the various historical societies alive and active."

"Yes?"

"Well, if I'm not mistaken, the Haddingtons are direct descendants of Faith Trevor Haddington."

Hope sat back down with a thud. "Are you sure?" Her voice sounded like a croak. "Are you absolutely sure?"

He bobbed his head, then placed his glasses back on the tip of his nose. "Oh, yes, dear. I'm sure. It's a shame they're not in town right now. I believe their youngest daughter just got married in St. Paul last week, and the family is still there."

So Faith *had* married! She hadn't waited for Armand, but had fallen in love with someone else! Hope leaned forward. "Do you know when they'll return?"

He shook his head. "Who can say? Tomorrow? A few days? Perhaps a week. Maybe by then you'll have found other information that might help."

She stood again, only this time her knees were weak. "Thank you again, Professor. I'll be here for a few days. Don't forget to call if you hear anything."

Hope left the spacious Victorian home and walked toward her car. She didn't have much information, but she did have hopes of getting some. And she now knew about Faith.

Mixed emotions flooded her as she thought about what the professor had said. On one hand, she was thrilled to death to find that Faith had been as fickle as she had thought her to be. On the other, she knew how much pain this information would cause Armand. Faith had been everything to him. . . .

Duluth was a fountain of information, but the sources were scattered all over. After another several hours at the public library, Hope found herself in the University of Minnesota library going through the archives, checking microfilmed bible flaps, letters and notes. There was nothing. Disappointment was a bitter taste in her mouth.

She trudged to the Northeast Historical Society's section. Most of the records there began in the 1850s, but there were a few mentions of the period she needed. Still she couldn't locate the names of the scouts.

Late that night, as she ate a meal from room service and listened to the news on TV, she had just about decided to call it quits and head back to the island. She'd rather be with Armand right now than sifting through reams of paper that were leading her nowhere.

The next morning she was certain that this trip was a wild-goose chase. All she could think of was getting back to Armand and the safety of his arms.

She packed quickly, throwing her things in the overnighter she had brought with her. She was just walking out the door when the telephone rang. She hesitated before answering it.

The professor's reedy voice made her heart beat faster. "I have some more information if you're still interested, Miss Langston. You can come over any time this morning, and I'll be glad to talk it over with you."

"Thank you, I'll be right there," she promised before hanging up. How stupid could she be? She had almost given up, which would have been disastrous for Armand. No matter how much she missed him, she had to keep searching.

8

"EVEN IF THEY ARE BACK from their trip, do you really think the Haddingtons have any more information about Faith Trevor?" Hope persisted. Leaning forward in her chair, she stared expectantly at the historian on the other side of the desk.

He squinted through his rimless glasses. "My dear, I would say that if anyone did, it would be Bella Haddington." He glanced down at his notes. "Faith was one of forty or fifty white women at Port Huron at the time, and most of them either married or went back to the cities scattered along the east coast. When they married, their own names were lost from the records." He wheezed. "But Faith Haddington is the exception, perhaps because she settled in the west rather than the east. I've spoken to Bella Haddington on the phone, and met her once or twice. She's a pleasure to talk to. Perhaps you could go by her home? I'm sorry I don't have the telephone number. I've misplaced it, and it's unlisted," he explained. "But if you knock at her door and tell her what you're doing, she might take time out of her busy schedule to see you."

Her face showed the doubt she felt. "You don't think she'd kick me off her property?"

He chuckled, reaching for a blank piece of paper and quickly scribbling down the address. "Bella doesn't seem the type of woman to turn anyone away." He pushed it across the desk. "It's worth a try."

She grinned. "It is, isn't it?" Suddenly she was excited. Perhaps she could piece this whole thing together, help find the information Armand needed to...

The professor interrupted her thoughts. "As for the other men, you've done very well on your own. Only one thing that mystifies me is the gentleman you can't locate. This Henri Houdon, I know he's in my records somewhere and I'm sure that I'll run across him. Just have patience," he said reassuringly. "I'll find him. My memory may not be as good as it used to be, but my notes are very thorough."

She smiled as she stood and held out her hand. "Thank you, Professor Richards. I can't tell you how much I appreciate this."

He brushed away her words with an arthritic hand and an answering smile. "No problem, as my grandchildren say. I'm only too happy to acquaint someone with their ancestors. It's that vital link between the past and the present that makes our future so much easier to bear."

"I agree." She smiled as she moved toward the door. It had been easier to tell him she was interested in her family's ancestors than to explain she had met a ghost who needed to piece his past together. Much easier. "May I come by tomorrow, before I leave Duluth?"

He nodded his balding head. "By all means. I know I'll have something by then, my dear." He glanced once more at the piles of paper on his desk. Hope was sure he was the only person who could possibly make sense out of that mess. She wasn't about to volunteer, much as she would have liked to dig around. She wanted answers and she needed them now, but prudence had to be her guide.

She let herself out. Glancing at her watch, she realized it was too early to make an impromptu call on a woman she had never met. Perhaps she should wait another hour or so.

Her step was light and almost bouncy as she made her way to the newspaper office. She still had a lot to learn. Even though there had been no newspapers in Armand's time, there had been pieces written during the thirties and forties about the colorful history of the area. Maybe one of those articles could help. One clue was all she needed.

The woman in charge threaded the spool of microfilm through the machine and left Hope to her task. Page by page, Hope checked through the papers, her interest piqued by the replay of day-to-day history. Armand had made those past days real to her. The people, places and events she was reading about seemed to belong to yesterday, not to a time two hundred years ago. The Indian wars, the trading posts that bought and shipped furs, the pemmican factories, the strange clothing and unusual household utensils—all had been part of the lives of those people who had carved a life out of the wilderness.

Suddenly one historical article caught her eye. Alongside the piece was a photograph of a portrait of a woman, blurred and faded, but clearly identifiable. She stared at the image for what seemed like hours, her heart racing. If it hadn't been for the hairstyle, it could have been herself.

The article was about Faith Trevor Haddington, who had married a British officer a year after Armand's death. Her husband had been forty-two, obviously much older than she, but they had built a lovely home in St. Paul and had had three children together, a son and two daughters. Faith had witnessed the changing of the boundaries from France to England and then to the United States during her lifetime of turmoil. She had lived to the ripe old age of sixty-two, the last ten years as a widow. Her descendants were scattered throughout Minnesota.

All the color left Hope's face as she read the article. Not only had Armand's love married, but she had had three children and had raised them nearby. Her pulse leaped in her throat and excitement coursed through her body.

Quickly calling back the librarian, she asked, "Are you familiar with this article?"

The librarian, a stocky lady in her mid-forties, bent toward the machine and squinted at the screen. Her face lit up with delight. "Ah, yes, Faith Haddington. She's quite a celebrity up here." Her voice became almost tender. "One of her descendants is a real VIP in Duluth. I'm sure you've heard of him. Jeff Haddington? He owns one of the most successful real-estate companies in the state, with an office here in Duluth that caters to clients wealthy enough to buy their own islands in the Boundary Waters Canoe Area," she said, referring to the land and water between the United States and Canada. "Not all of that land is national park, you know."

Hope nodded. "I know," she said absently. No wonder the name was familiar. Her father had often recommended that her mother sell the island through Jeff Haddington. And Bella Haddington was his mother. Now that she thought of it, she vaguely remembered her mother having been an acquaintance of Mrs. Haddington.

"And Mrs. Haddington has generously donated a wealth of research material to the library. She's a wonderful woman."

"Does she live with her son?"

"Why, I believe she does." The librarian smiled.

Hope pointed to the screen. "May I have a copy of this article?"

"Of course. Just put a quarter in the slot, push that button, and the machine will do it."

Hope did as she was told, and a small white copy came out of the side of the machine. As she folded it and put it in her purse, she asked one more question. "Is Jeff Haddington still here?"

The woman nodded. "Oh, yes. He travels some, but his home is the one at the edge of town, toward French Harbor. His family was in the mining industry here when they built it. You know, the red brick one with the tall wrought-iron fence around it that sits on the side of the mountain overlooking Lake Superior? It's a beautiful place, the finest in the Arrowhead area, some say."

"I'm sure it is," Hope said, picking up her notebook. "Thank you very much, you've been a great help. I'll be back tomorrow."

Fifteen minutes later she was on the road that would take her to the Haddington residence. She thought of the article and the picture that had brought her face-to-face with herself. For the first time since she had seen the article, she thought about Armand. He had mistaken Hope for Faith. She finally understood why.

It wasn't just that she looked like a carbon copy of Faith that shook her. It was that Armand had become hers—her man, her property. Now she had to face that fact with knowledge that was earth-shattering to her.

She loved him; she had told him so. But now she doubted he could tell the difference between her and the woman he had loved so many years ago. Earlier today, the ground beneath her had been solid, despite the fact that Armand was a ghost. Now, with the discovery of her picture and the basic facts about Faith's life, she was once more unsure of everything.

One message did come through, and it was one she had already suspected, but hadn't really believed until this moment. Armand had fallen in love with Hope because she looked like Faith, not because she was Hope. That knowledge was shattering to her.

The enormous, dark red brick home sat on the edge of the cliff, deep green grounds and a tall wrought-iron fence surrounding its several acres. If the house hadn't been so beautiful, it could have been used as a setting for a Gothic novel. Luckily the gates were open, and Hope drove in, her hands clenching the steering wheel. She prayed there were answers waiting for her at the end of the drive.

Her courage almost deserted her when she stood in front of the large double doors. It was only by sheer willpower that she remained where she was and waited for the chime to be answered. And when it was, her voice deserted her.

"Yes?" An older woman with beautifully graying hair pulled back in a ponytail stood in the entryway. She wore jeans, a jade-green silk shirt and dangling earrings. Though she was obviously in her late fifties, she was in great shape for any age.

"Mrs. Haddington?" Hope asked finally.

"Yes, how can I help you?"

"I was wondering if you could talk to me about Faith Trevor Haddington. I'm doing some research for an article about women who helped settle this area, and ran across her name."

The older woman's eyes narrowed, taking in every nuance of Hope's face, obviously seeing the resemblance. "Are you a relative?"

Hope smiled, pulling out her wallet and showing her press card for *Today's World* magazine. "No, but I've been told I look like her." *By a ghost who loves her very much.*

Mrs. Haddington's expression relaxed. "Of course. You're Cynthia Langston's daughter! I met her several times when she came to visit the island. Teardrop, isn't it?"

"Yes," Hope said, relieved that this was going to be easier than she had thought.

"I was sorry to hear she had died. She dearly loved this part of the country. Almost as much as I do."

"I know. In fact, I use it as home base when I'm writing."

Bella Haddington stood back. "Well, no use yakking on the steps. Come in, and I'll see if I can help." She led the way into a high-ceilinged library whose glass cases ran around the entire room. "Faith was a remarkable woman, you know."

"Was she? How so?" Hope asked, taking a seat on one of the twin sofas bordering the large fireplace.

"She married a British officer her father chose for her, raised three children on land that wasn't to become St. Paul until almost a hundred years later. When her husband died, she continued the family shipping business until her son was old enough to take over."

"She had three children, didn't she?"

"Yes, a boy and two girls. The boy was my great-great-grandfather."

Hope cleared her voice, asking a question that had been sitting in the back of her mind. "Was he tall?"

Mrs. Haddington laughed. "Goodness, no! Back in those days, men weren't as tall as they are now. And besides, I think the colonel, the man Faith married, was shorter than average. I believe father and son were very much alike."

"How do you know?"

"Why..." The older woman's well-arched eyebrows rose over mischievous eyes. "Didn't you know? I have her journal. She wrote in it faithfully. Every day until her death."

"Would it... is there any way I could see it?" Hope asked, her heart tripping over itself. Would it mention Armand? Would it give a clue as to whether or not Faith had been waiting for him in Port Huron?

Mrs. Haddington shook her head. "I'm afraid we have the journal sealed to keep it from deteriorating any further. You can imagine how the humidity here would eat at it."

Hope hid her disappointment. One road block after another. "Yes. Certainly."

The older woman stood. "But I do have a typewritten copy of it, if you'd care to see that. It's not as good as holding the original, but at least you can read it."

"I'd love to!" Hope stood, too, tracing her hostess's steps to the large table in one corner of the library.

Everything in the room faded as Hope began her journey into Faith's diary. It began on her first day in her new home along the Mississippi, on the land that would become St. Paul. Three hours later, with tears almost blinding her as they streamed down her cheeks, she read the last entry.

I know now that youth is made for fools, middle age for guilt and old age for regrets. My regret is sometimes too strong for me to overcome. My soldier, my soldier. Gone forever and it was my fault. I often wonder, now that life's pace has slowed to a snail's walk and I have time to do nothing but think, what could have happened if Father had not become ill that fateful night, and I had left Port Huron? Is he happy now? Does he have the children he so wanted? Does he miss me?

There were several pages about the children and grandchildren. Then one last paragraph.   *I met a young half-breed trader named Santeuil today. When I questioned him on his name, he explained his heritage. He also told me that his uncle must have died years ago, for he never returned to France or tried to reach his brother again. The sorrow is almost unbearable. All these years of wondering about another's happiness only to find death. But perhaps death is the final peace. Perhaps it is the meeting place of like minds and loves. Perhaps.*

"Now don't you start!" Bella Haddington strode into the room balancing a tray filled with glasses, a pitcher, and a plate of sandwiches. "Every time I get to the end, I start to blubber, too. It's such a tragic story, isn't it?"

Hope closed the notebook. "But how did she survive all that hatred that must have surrounded her? Her husband sounds like a monster!"

"Well, I have my own theory." She poured tea into the ice-filled glasses and handed one to Hope. "I think he always knew that Faith was in love with another man. A soldier, as far as I can tell. I think it ate at him, and he took it out on her. He never abused her physically, just ignored her unless he could say something caustic in public. And from what Faith says, he was very good at embarrassing her."

Hope leaned back and wiped her eyes, slightly embarrassed to be sitting in this woman's library crying. "But why commit suicide? She was free of him by then!"

"I'm not sure, but from Faith's point of view, she was old, and all used up. She lived under the unbearably heavy umbrella of guilt and regrets, all making for a very unhappy woman. When she found out that her true love was probably dead, the last of her dreams was shattered. I think she thought she could join him."

"Only she didn't," Hope whispered.

Bella Haddington shrugged. "How do we know? I've lived long enough to know that anything in this crazy world is possible."

Hope reached for her tea again, unable even to look at the sandwiches. Her stomach was churning already. "Do you know the names of any men who worked for Faith's husband?"

"One or two. Why?"

"I was just wondering." She rummaged in her purse and pulled out the three scouts' names. "Do any of these look familiar?"

Bella accepted the list and scanned the names. Her brow furrowed as she studied each one. "No, not offhand." She looked up, her brown eyes pinning Hope. "But you might try a Professor Richards in Duluth. He

seems to know everything about everyone, and is a delightful man to talk with. You might also try several of
the historical homes in the city. A few are museums
now, and offer a wealth of information."

) "Thank you." Hope stood, her hand outstretched.
"And thank you for allowing me to read Faith's diary.
It was just what I was looking for," she said, referring
to the story she had given when she had entered Mrs.
Haddington's home.

The woman's laughter was almost girlish. "I enjoyed
it. My son says that I could talk about our family history all day long for a year and wouldn't run out of tid-
bits of information. And he's right."

They walked to the front door slowly, stopping just
before they reached the center of the large entryway.
Mrs. Haddington pointed to a framed painting on the
wall. "This is Faith Trevor Haddington. It's no wonder
I thought you were a relation."

A portrait of Faith was sealed inside the glass,
cracked and slightly faded with age, but clear just the
same. She must have been around thirty when this one
had been made, and a tragic sadness seemed to ema-
nate from the smile on her face. "She was beautiful,
wasn't she?" Hope said softly, seeing the vulnerability
in her eyes and the hope in the uptilt of her lips.

"So are you, my dear," Mrs. Haddington replied,
equally softly. "Let me know if I can help you in any
other way."

"I will," Hope promised; then she walked through the
portals and to her car. As she slid behind the wheel, she
saw another car approaching the house from the long
drive. She drove away slowly, watching the other car
take her place in the driveway.

ALL NIGHT LONG she tossed and turned, unable to let Faith's story go. Even though she hadn't been outside the fort at the appointed time, Faith had wanted to be with Armand after all. She hadn't been too young to know what was in her heart, just too young to do anything about it.

And that almost broke Hope's heart.

The next morning, she rinsed her face in cold water, splashing her wrists and throat, too. Her toothbrush got the best working of its life as she scrubbed away. If only her feelings of inadequacy could be scrubbed away, as well....

Not quite a month ago she had met a ghost, and he had turned her life, her thoughts and her beliefs topsy-turvy. Had she fallen in love with him because he was a ghost, and that made him a safe risk? Or was it because he was so caring, so loving, so very real to her? She didn't know.

According to what she'd read in the diary, Faith had been a pretty but flighty young lady, who wasn't willing to sacrifice everything in order to love her man. Then she had paid a heavy price for that shallow thinking by having to live with a man who was a harsh taskmaster.

Her hand dropped slowly to the sink. What difference did any of it make? No matter what happened, or what Armand felt, she had to help him put his soul to rest. And the time was coming when she would have to leave the island. The winters up here came early, the snow and ice and cold were pure Arctic. The house wouldn't help Armand, thanks to that damnable invisible wall. The cold would trap his soul, too, just as the land did. And she would be gone by then, unable to help anymore. There was no alternative. She had to help him now, even though she knew by doing so she would lose him.

She grabbed her purse and left the room. She still had to ask the professor a few more questions.

THE PROFESSOR RUFFLED through his papers. "I believe I told you yesterday that I recognized one of the names. Well, I was right. Tourbet was a voyageur in these parts, a French soldier at one time who decided that providing pelts to France was a much better way to earn a living. His family, offspring from a beautiful Indian maiden, married others at the fort, and before long the family moved to Minneapolis. Now the family is in North Carolina in the tobacco industry."

"I see," Hope said, taking it all in and trying to assimilate his words in the presence of a growling stomach. She should have eaten something before she came. "Have you ever heard anything about a brass-bound chest? Or a key, an ivory key? I believe it was a keepsake he owned that was about six inches long, intricately carved, and the handle was bound with brass thread."

The professor frowned. "No, I don't believe so. It doesn't sound familiar, but that doesn't mean anything. My mind isn't what it once was." He stared at her through his thick glasses. "Is this key important?"

Hope smiled. "I don't really know. But one of my ancestors had one, and it was a family keepsake. It may be that when I find the key, I'll find my relatives."

"I see," he nodded slowly. "Sort of like a seal that makes it official. A confirmation of sorts."

Hope smiled. "Yes, sort of."

"Well, I'll certainly keep it in mind for those other fellows you asked me about. If I find anything, I'll let you know." He glanced down at the file folder in front of him. "I have your address."

"Yes, but my mail is delivered here, and I come in once a week to pick it up. If you'll just put a note in my box, as soon as I get it I'll come over right away."

"Very well." His eyes took on a faraway look; obviously, he was eager to get back to his studies. "But I won't promise anything. Even my own research leaves much to be desired. I'm scarcely halfway through."

"I'm sure," Hope soothed as she edged toward the door. She needed a history lesson, but only on the period that pertained to her search. "I'm very grateful for your help."

But he was already lost in examining a scribbled piece of paper in front of him.

She spent half an hour reaching the family in North Carolina. But when she did, it was a dead end. No one had ever heard of an ivory key. And no one in the family particularly cared...

When she retrieved the mail, she shoved it into her purse unopened. She picked up her car and drove to the grocery store, then to the island.

She might as well get past the initial meeting with Armand, telling him about the tobacco family and Faith's marriage. Her stomach did a little flip again, and a flush heated her face. As long as she didn't think about Faith, she could function. But the thought of the other woman made her ill with jealousy. She had never been jealous before in her life, but then she had never been this much in love either. She hated it!

ARMAND STOOD on the shore several yards from the dock, the binoculars Hope had given him resting on his chest. His hands were perched almost arrogantly on his hips as he watched her angle the small craft toward him. The moment he had heard its engine pop to life, his heart had soared with both relief and love. She was all right; nothing had happened, he kept reassuring himself. But even though Hope had returned, apparently in one piece, something was wrong. From a distance he could see the worried look in her eyes. The gray pallor of her face matched her outfit. What had happened?

"What is it?" he asked solicitously as he helped her out of the boat, ignoring the boxes of groceries stacked on the seat. "What happened?"

"Nothing," she said. "I'll explain later."

He clasped her shoulders, holding her directly in front of him as he stared into her eyes. "Now. You will tell me now."

His command was just the spark she needed to set off her anger. Her eyes flashed up at him, and her body went rigid in his hands. "After we get those boxes off the boat and put away."

"Tell me," he said coaxingly, his strong hands leaving her shoulders to cup her slim neck and chin as he stared tenderly into her vulnerable face.

She closed her eyes against the loving look he was bestowing upon her, knowing now, beyond a doubt, that she was only a stand-in for the woman whose picture was in her purse.

"It has to do with Faith," he guessed. Hope flinched.

"Yes." She straightened her spine, then slumped. "I discovered that Faith married a man just one year after you died, and that she had three children. She lived to the ripe old age of sixty-two."

"Who was he?" His voice was a monotone, his hand clutching hers painfully.

"A British officer. Charles Haddington."

He spit out an expletive, and she winced as his hand tightened. Suddenly he let her go, covering his face with both hands as he tried to control himself. When he looked up, his expression was as bleak as a hard winter's storm. "That man was the most pompous ass I ever met. Faith used to stand clear of him for fear that would happen."

Hope didn't know what to say, so she nodded.

"She did not like him from the moment they met. At a dance at the fort, I believe."

She nodded again, knotting her hands in her lap when she really wanted to stroke the side of his jaw, brush back that lock of onyx hair that continued to fall on his forehead. Comfort him, she told herself, but the cold, angry look in his eyes kept her at bay.

At last he sighed, his shoulders relaxing. "I knew she would have to marry. I just did not expect it would be to a bastard like Haddington. She must have lived a terrible life."

His sympathetic response to Faith's predicament acted like gasoline to a spark. Hope quickly began packing a few provisions into a box, carelessly slamming packages from one into the other.

"Hope! What are you doing?" His hands touched her waist as she bent over a box. She twisted around until he was forced to let her go.

"Nothing," she said thickly. "I'm just going down to the house. I need to do a few things, and you need some time by yourself. This will be better, believe me."

"No!" His denial boomed across the top of the hill, echoing across the lake and stopping her cold. He took a deep breath. "I am sorry, but I do not want you to go anywhere. You are here. You will remain here."

Her anger flared. "To do what? Watch you ache for a woman who didn't have guts enough to go after what she wanted? A woman who didn't love you enough to fight for you?" She gave a bitter laugh. "No, thanks. I'm no masochist, and I won't be a substitute."

He smiled at her fury. "You never were a substitute."

She knelt in front of him, her knees giving way as the anger bled from her. Her breast still heaved and ached with emotion. "Yes, I was. You said I looked exactly like her, and you were right! No wonder you thought you loved me, thought that I was Faith!"

"How do you know?"

She rummaged through her purse looking for the article she had copied, spilling the contents before she found it. "Here!" she cried, handing him the paper. "There's a picture of her." She gave a nervous laugh again as he slowly took the copy from her shaking hands. "Then I saw the original. Except for the hairdo, we'd be twins!"

With painstaking thoroughness, Armand stared at the picture before looking back at her with eyes that told her the whole story. "You do look very much alike. Your souls are just as kind, too. But in—how do you say it?—personality, you are two very different women. Faith would never have dared to oppose me, to inject an opinion into a conversation, to love me with an abandon that reveals true love." He glanced down at the article, then back at Hope. "The woman of my idealistic youth is here, on this paper. The woman I love as a grown man loves is right in front of me."

"I read her diary, Armand. She was a shallow woman in her youth, and a bitter, regretful woman in her later years. But we look so much alike, it's frightening." Tears shimmered in her eyes. "And I don't think you can tell us apart."

Slowly he nodded, his eyes piercing hers. "Oh, but I can, Hope. Never doubt that." His arms encircled her shoulders to clasp her tightly, so that she was pressed against him from shoulders to hips. His warm hands tried to stroke feeling into her back and hips and absorb her at the same time. The message his body sent was clear. His love. His darling.

He didn't realize that the two brief thoughts had been said aloud until suddenly she was crying, sobbing into the curve of his neck as if her heart were shattered. Firm, gentle hands touched her, heated her, comforted her. Words that were barely whispers passed from his soft, warm mouth into her ear. His strong, firm body pressed hard against her, reminding her of other times when he had held her like this because he had wanted her. Needed her.

Then they were kissing, as if it was their first and last kiss, and those dormant sensations he was able to arouse so easily flooded through her. She forced her body closer against his, longing to climb right inside him, to be protected by him. Loved by him. Consumed by him. How could Faith not have loved him enough to battle for the right to stand at his side!

Her hands clasped his head as she returned kiss for kiss. She stopped breathing to be one with him, so as not to lose this connection that was as vital to her as sun and air and water. Her lips trailed along his jaw, drawing succor from his very pores.

His callused hands were under her sweater, eliminating the first barrier between them. The snap of her slacks gave way under his tug as she lay down, and he lay on top of her, neither willing to lose contact, even for a second.

Her fingers worked at the buttons of his pants, as impatient with him as he had been with her, because she needed him just as much.

His lips sought her breast, his searing breath reaching her tender nipple before his tongue and mouth found its firming softness. A low moan echoed from her throat as he raised his hips and plunged all the way into her in a single shattering stroke, his heated body shoving her against the earth.

They loved each other with a primal ferocity they had not felt before. Her eyes closed as feelings as heavy as he was began to infiltrate her very core. They were alive! This moment was the proof of it, her mind cried. Then she couldn't think at all. Her face glowed, her eyes widened to stare into the tender but frightening blue depths of his as he gave a final thrust to bring them as close as two people could be.

Time stopped. She had no idea how long it took her to float back to earth, clinging to his shoulders with shaking fingers.

His smile was so tender it brought tears to her eyes. "*Ma petite*," he breathed as he stroked strands of her hair away from her face. "I love you so very much."

She tried to swallow, but the emotions that were welling up inside her wouldn't allow her to do so. He kissed her forehead, then rolled to her side, his hand still caressing her waist. They lay that way in silence for a long time, but at last Armand propped himself on one elbow and looked down at her.

His expression changed from tender and loving to puzzled as his gaze shifted to a spot just beyond her left shoulder. "You are not opening your post, *chérie*?" he asked.

Hope glanced over her shoulder to see what he was referring to. For a moment she was confused. Then a smile teased the corners of her mouth as she saw her spilled purse and the scattered letters. "It's from my father," she answered, gradually releasing her fingers from their grip on his shoulders.

Armand grinned sheepishly. "Of course. A doting father. I should have guessed."

Her smile faded. "You guessed wrong. My father has never been doting."

"Then why else would he bother to write you two letters in one week?"

Hope's heart actually stopped at his words, only to begin beating in double time. Something was wrong. She sat up and with shaking hands sorted through the letters and bills she had not even bothered to look at earlier.

Armand was right. There were two letters from her father, not typed on his usual formal stationery, but posted in plain envelopes and addressed in his own forceful hand.

9

HOPE QUICKLY SCANNED her father's letters. The first said he was coming to visit her in order to judge the state of her health for himself. She closed her eyes for a moment and tried to remain calm. All she needed now was a monkey wrench in the works. Didn't she have enough to do with Armand fading faster every day? She shouldn't have to handle a "concerned" father, too.

His second letter announced the day he would arrive and that he would stay only two days because of pressing business. Pressing business? He *hated* the island and wouldn't be coming at all if he'd his druthers! She was surprised he was staying even that long.

Her state of health? Thanks to Armand, it had never been better. Besides, she could have sworn that her father had been affected more by his secretary's death than by Hope's experience in Central America. She shook her head, rejecting the thought. No, that wasn't fair. Though Hope and her father were separated by a distance of minds, he wasn't a monster. But while she had accepted that they would never meet on common ground to share any of the intangibles, apparently her father wasn't yet willing to acknowledge defeat. He probably wanted reassurance of her mental stability so he could relax and go about his own business. To him, appearances were everything.

Armand watched her as she scanned the letters a second time. "We are to be separated again."

"No," she said, reaching over to place her fingers over his lips, then lingering to caress them. "My father is visiting me to make sure I'm all right. He'll sleep in the house, and I'll sleep in the tent. With you."

His breath whispered across her cheek with a warmth that reached deep. "Are you certain?"

"Yes. I just have to straighten up the house and get cleaned up. He's arriving soon." Her fingers drifted down the side of his face to trace the strong jaw, and she reveled in the sensation of the stubbly roughness of his day-old beard on her palm. No matter what happened, she and Armand would spend the rest of his time here together. She had him now, but too soon he'd be gone, and then all she'd have would be the memories they created today.

"I worry about you," Armand said softly. "Your lovely eyes show a growing strain, and I know I do not have the power to erase it."

She smiled. "I'm fine."

"I love you, Hope. You know that now, do you not?"

Her smile widened, warming him. "Yes," she repeated. "I know that . . . now."

"It will work out."

She couldn't answer that. She didn't know if he was right.

SHE HAD JUST FINISHED applying her makeup when she heard the whine of a motor. Grabbing her brush, she pulled it through her hair once more, then caught the sides and held them back with tortoiseshell combs. A quick glance in the mirror showed her she looked almost as good as new. She had even gained back some of her weight. Her father would have to say the island convalescence had agreed with her. She smiled, for it was really Armand who agreed with her, body and soul.

When the skiff pulled into the dock, she was standing on the pier, relaxed, and with a big smile still lighting her face.

Her father, wearing white flannel trousers and a white-and-blue polo shirt, jumped off. He was as good-looking as ever. The touch of gray at his temples set off his dark hair, the only gene they seemed to share. He was trim, his face strong and square, his expression slightly intimidating. But his eyes, normally a cool gray, were filled with concern as he examined her closely. Then he strode toward her, enfolding her in a bear hug that made her remember her childhood.

"You look good, honey," he said gruffly. "Still a little peaked, but a lot better than a month ago."

"Thanks for the seal of approval." She grinned at him.

His own smile dropped. "I said you looked good, not completely well. Central America took its toll."

She placed a kiss on his cheek, surprised at the tenderness he was showing. This was a side of him she hadn't seen since she was a child. "What *about* Central America?" she teased. "I don't remember a thing." She realized, surprised, that it was true. It wasn't important to her anymore.

Her father retrieved a box tied with rope, and carrying it with one hand, he placed his other arm around her shoulders. Together they walked up the path to the house.

Just then a whistle caught her attention. Quickly, she scanned the trees to her left. There he was, his hands on his hips, lounging against one of the pines, whistling that damned tune of his as he watched them, the twinkle in his eyes visible even from the path.

Her heartbeat raced as she realized he was in full view of her father. She shook her head in warning, but he just shrugged his shoulders and continued whistling.

"What is it, honey? What's wrong?" Her father stopped, staring down at her. "Are you in pain? Are you dizzy?"

"Oh, no," she managed to stutter. "I'm fine. Really I just stepped on a stone, and it skittered across another one and I didn't know what it was." She bent down, pretending to look at the offending pebbles. As her father followed her gaze, she stretched her arm out to the side and gestured at Armand, attempting to shoo him into the woods.

Her signal must have worked, because the whistling stopped. She straightened, a bright, vacuous smile on her lips, to find her father staring at her as if she had just eluded the guards in an asylum.

He touched the back of his hand to her forehead. "Are you all right?" He asked the question carefully, but his eyes showed concern—or was it fear lurking there? Fear for her sanity?

A giggle erupted. At least Frank hadn't heard her ghost! "I'm fine, really," she managed, but the thought of how she must have appeared to him made her break up again. "Something just hit my funny bone. That's all."

"I see," he said slowly, confused at her behavior. They began walking toward the house once more. "At least you haven't lost your sense of humor."

Hope laughed aloud in sheer relief. "Not lately. It's alive and well, Frank."

His only reply was a grunt that suggested he didn't believe a word she'd said.

She opened the screen door and led him into the kitchen. "How about a cup of tea, or something to eat?"

"No, thanks." He lifted the box. "I brought my own food. A little restaurant I stopped at along the way left a lot to be desired, but I did eat something."

She could imagine. There was only a country café between the lake and Two Harbors, and it served plain, home-style cooking. No French chefs, no gourmet dishes, just good, hearty fare that would fill a hungry working man's stomach—not to her father's epicurean taste at all.

She couldn't resist baiting him. "Some folks think it's the best restaurant around," she said, setting the kettle on the stove to warm up the pot of tea she had made earlier.

"I have no doubt some 'folks' would. But it wasn't quite to my liking. I want my fish broiled, not fried." His dour expression said more than words could, and laughter lit Hope's eyes again.

After her tea was made they sat quietly on the front steps of the porch, each waiting for the other to speak. Her father cleared his throat. She cocked her head toward him, curious about what he had on his mind. He was nervous, but the Frank Langston she knew was never nervous about anything. "Hope," he began slowly, "I want you to come home with me. Spend some time in Washington. Relax."

She placed a hand on his arm. He cared for her, she knew. He just didn't know how to show it. He never had. Still, he had come all this way... "Thanks, Frank," she said softly, giving his arm a squeeze. "I appreciate your concern, but I'm fine."

"I don't like the idea of your staying here alone. It's too dangerous."

"I was visiting you when I was kidnapped," she reminded him mildly. "Besides, Washington is your home. *This* is mine."

"It's that damn career of yours," he growled, letting out the frustration that had gnawed at him all the way to Minnesota. "It's too damned dangerous. If it weren't for that job, you'd be married, taking care of a house full of children instead of traipsing all over the globe."

She raised her eyebrows haughtily. She wasn't Frank Langston's daughter for nothing. "Is that what you think all women were born for? Or just me, because I'm lucky enough to be your daughter?"

"Don't you try that tone with me, young lady. I'm a past master at turning the tables." He straightened. "I not only think your job is dangerous, I think you ought to consider another alternative to this, this, crude lifestyle." With a wave of his hand he encompassed the entire island.

Hope knew exactly what he meant. "I think I've heard this argument before. Several times, in fact." She turned to face him, her eyes shooting darts at him. "Wasn't this much the same thing you used to say to mother? *Before* she divorced you to become one of the best computer programmers in the business?"

Even the birds stopped singing. Her father's face stiffened and turned gray at the accusation. "That's dirty, Hope."

"You bet it is. Just about as dirty as you trying to keep me seventeen." Her bitterness overflowed. "Remember that year, Frank? It was the year mother died, and you tried to keep me out of my first year in college because you thought I ought to recuperate from mother's death. What you really wanted was an obedient daughter who could learn to play hostess to half of Washington." Her breath caught in her throat, turning into a lump of cold hard anger. "And you couldn't even go to the damn funeral!"

"I had an ulcer attack!" He defended himself. "And it was also the year that you, in one of your childish fits, began calling me Frank instead of Dad."

They stared at each other through the deepening twilight for long minutes, each measuring the pain of the other at last. Then all the fight drained from Hope's body. She stared at the calm blue water. "Hell and damnation," she said calmly.

The cicadas were warming up for their nightly serenade, and the sound of the water lapping at the dock could be heard clearly before her father spoke again. "I loved her, you know. I loved her so much I wanted her to be with me all the time."

"But not enough to let her go." Her control was on a tightwire. She didn't want to see his hurt and guilt. "You wanted to bundle her and me in wrapping paper and stick us in a closet so whenever the urge to be a father and husband came over you, we'd be there, waiting like a good little family should."

"You don't know what you're talking about," he said wearily. "It takes two people to make a marriage."

"Just as it took two to produce me. But only one of you had the time or desire to look after me." A trace of bitterness seeped into her voice. "So don't bother handling out platitudes at this stage. I think I've heard them all."

"Perhaps, with hindsight, you might be right. But our marriage failure still had nothing to do with you and is not a topic for discussion. You're only bringing up your mother as a red herring to divert my attention from you."

"Your marriage had everything to do with me. I was the one in the middle." She gulped a deep breath and let it out slowly. "Besides, you were the one who brought up your marriage," she corrected. "I had already turned down your offer and had moved on to something else."

"Then let's stick to the topic I originally chose," he said reasonably, ignoring the brief flare-up between them. "I want you to come back with me to Washington for a few weeks. Please. After that, we'll see."

"Why?"

"Do you honestly believe you've recovered completely from that ordeal in Central America?" Frank's voice was soft, and she became wary.

Hope stood and took two steps to the ground, jamming her hands into the back pockets of her jeans as she swiveled slowly to face him. She couldn't leave Armand. Not now. "I want to enjoy your visit, Frank, but I can't when I know you came here to talk me into leaving. I just want you to accept my decision. I'm not going. I'm staying here until the time is right for me to leave. Then I'll come visit you."

The battle of wills was evident even in the darkness. They stared at each other, determination etching their faces, until finally her father stared down at the steps. She gave a deep sigh of relief. Too soon.

"There's another reason you need to come with me," he said softly. A shiver went down her spine. "The Senate Foreign Affairs Committee wants you to testify. They're reviewing our Central American policies, especially Sao Jimenez, and they want your input. In fact, they demand it."

"And you knew this all along." Her words were barely a whisper.

"Yes."

"Then this trip is because of that, isn't it?" Where was the surprise she should have felt? "You let me believe that you were concerned only for my health. My welfare."

"Because I am. Your health comes first, no matter what. The hearings are three weeks from now, and I wanted you to have a few weeks of rest before you had to face them. If you were a housewife, Hope, you wouldn't have been in this mess to begin with. *That's* why I wished you hadn't been a career woman. A career cuts everything else out of life, including the happy moments. I know." His eyes closed in pain. "Loving moments can't be born when both people are totally involved in a career."

Hope turned and stared out at the dark mound of earth to the side of the house, wanting nothing more than to be enfolded in Armand's protective arms. She needed his soothing touch, his quiet, reassuring whisper. His strength.

"Hope. I tried to get your name off the list," he said. "But I'm not that powerful. Whether or not you had to appear, I wanted you home with me for a while."

She sighed, knowing he probably did. "Don't worry, Frank. I'll stand in front of the committee. But my choice is to stay here until I have to leave."

"Don't I have any say in the matter?"

Her voice was filled with conviction. "No."

"You're my daughter, Hope. I was hoping . . ." His voice trailed off.

"So was I. At one time I thought we could be friends, if not family."

"Don't say that." His voice was actually trembling. Real or an act? She couldn't say, but wouldn't trust her emotions.

"If I had my way, Frank," she said slowly, "I wouldn't be saying anything to you because you wouldn't be here. You'd be in Washington sending me wish-you-were-here cards and minding your own business. Just like the old days . . ." Years of bitter, weary anger spilled out, dampening her soul with tears.

"My God. How very harsh and judgmental you are."

Without a word, Hope turned and slowly entered the house. Her father followed her down the narrow hallway.

They spent the rest of the evening making safe, superficial conversation. The food was delicious, but all Hope could think about was how she could get some of it up to Armand. After what he had been eating, the food her father brought would make Armand's day.

"Hope?" Her father finally raised his voice, apparently having a hard time getting her attention.

She flushed guiltily. "Yes?"

"Which is my room?" His tone was patient, but his body was slumped slightly over the table and he was leaning on his elbows.

For the first time in a very long while, Hope took a good look at her father. She hadn't really noticed the dark sienna circles beneath his eyes or the pinched look of strain around his mouth. And the slightly pained squint was a recent and undesirable development. Time had taken its toll. He looked exhausted. When had he grown old, and why was she just now noticing it? Perhaps she had been just as blind as her father...

She shook her head. "You can use the spare bedroom. It's already made up for you. I'll be sleeping outside tonight."

"You'll do no such thing. For heaven's sake, you need your rest more than anyone."

"There's no need for concern. I have a tent at the top of the hill where I've been sleeping very comfortably. I'd rather sleep up there than in the house," she said stiffly.

He looked as if he was going to argue the point, then decided against it. "Then I'll say good-night," he replied, turning toward the narrow staircase.

Hope let out a sigh of relief. "Good night," she answered as he disappeared up the stairs.

In fifteen minutes she had the kitchen cleaned. It was the longest fifteen minutes Hope had ever spent.

Every muscle railed against pulling her up the hill. But her head and her heart told her that Armand would be near. Dear Lord, there was so little time left.

"I was becoming worried, little one." Armand's velvety voice came from behind the small pine. She jumped at the sound. Her eyes searched the area, trying to spot his tall, well-formed shape. She had been so intent on reaching the top, she had forgotten to look for him at the barrier. He was sitting on the incline, legs bent, his arms resting across his knees as he faced the house and the path.

The side of his face was lit by moonlight, making the rest of him resemble the devil incarnate. His hair was like pitch, and eyes that glowed like silver-blue coal stared at her. Was there ever a face as handsome or as devastating as his?

She let go of all the tension, now that she had reached her goal. "I couldn't get away immediately."

His chuckle was as dark and deep as his demonic appearance. "I could tell." He held out his hand to her, palm up, silently beckoning her to join him.

"How?" she asked, moving toward him. She ducked down and cuddled next to his warmth.

He chuckled again as he wrapped her sweetly in the warmth of his arm, just where she needed to be. "I know the daughter. She was probably very busy arguing," he answered. "But for right now, my Hope, let me enjoy the black-and-silver beauty of the night." He gazed up at the star-speckled sky. "It is so peaceful here."

"Umm," she murmured, snuggling closer into the heat of his body. She leaned her head on his shoulder. It was firm but padded. A perfect pillow, she sighed in sleepy contentment. But his next question woke her right up.

"Your father seems to be a reasonable man. I do not understand why you were so worried about his visit."

"Reasonable? He's trying to blackmail me into going back to Washington with him. Immediately! And you helped him along by making me look like a crazy woman!" she whispered angrily. "For a moment I felt like the Mad Hatter at a tea party!"

"Do you still have them?" he asked, his warm breath stimulating the sensitive side of her neck.

"Have what?"

"Mad hatters. Our hatters used to go insane from breathing the fine beaver hair with which they made the stylish hats," he explained patiently. "Do people still wear those hats? I have not seen any on the people in the magazines."

She gave a tired chuckle. "At least now I know where the saying originated, but no, we don't wear them anymore, even though we use the expression." She rubbed her chin against his chest.

"Why does he want you to visit his home? You said the man was your father, but you call him by his Christian name."

"It started a long time ago," she explained defensively. But for the first time since her mother died, she had cause to wonder if she wasn't acting like a child, as her father had charged. It had started that way, she knew, but as time passed it became too awkward to change back.

She felt the tension in Armand's shoulder and arm muscles slowly ease. "I think I am beginning to understand you, my Hope. And, for some reason, that worries me more than anything else." He sighed resignedly, one hand stroking the tender, soft skin of her breast before standing and pulling her up after him. "Come. I think it is time you slept." His arm circled her waist as he led her up the hill. Her head still rested against his chest, her hand in his. "I want you lying next to me, where I know you are safe."

"I am safe," she said finally, balancing on tiptoe to kiss the sharp angle of his jaw. "And I'm happy. Very happy."

He pulled her into his arms and kissed her forehead. "So am I, my lovely one. So am I."

The moon traveled across the bright, starry sky, but Hope didn't notice it. She was where she wanted to be—safe in Armand's arms.

And, with morning's light, she could pretend he wasn't fading, even though it was happening more and more lately. The process seemed to be accelerating as she gleaned more information.

She was damned if she did, and damned if she didn't.

"HOW A CHILD OF MINE could be so stubborn!" Her father had his arms crossed sternly over his chest. His brown eyes blazed with anger and frustration.

Calmly Hope took another sip of her morning coffee. "I don't know one other person on this earth who could match you for stubbornness. Just look at the genes. They'll tell the story every time."

"Don't you get smart with me, young lady. I'm still your father!"

"Nobody's denying that." She reached for the jar of fresh plum jam he'd brought and began spreading some on her whole-wheat toast. "But you're not my guardian. I'm staying until the hearing begins."

Frank's eyes narrowed, but his voice softened. "Please travel with me. I came up here because I wanted to get to know you better—something we would have done years ago if it weren't for that stupid Langston pride of ours." Hesitantly, he touched her hand.

Though he was clearly reaching out to her as he never had before, she couldn't respond—at least, not as he wanted her to. Armand was in the way, and Hope could not do to him what Faith had done. Hope refused to choose her father over Armand. "I can't. Not right now, at least. Please give me more time."

He stiffened first, then slumped. The hand that had touched hers fell into his lap. "You won't make yes an answer, no matter what I say, will you?"

She shook her head slowly. "I'm sorry, but I can't. Give me two weeks. Just two weeks, and then I'll go to Washington."

"One. You'll need one more to get ready for the committee."

"Two," she repeated. "Your staff is competent, and I won't have much to say to the committee, anyway."

His eyes gleamed ruefully. "Honey, you bargain like a seasoned political pro." There was a hint of admiration in his eyes. "Perhaps you missed your calling."

She grinned. "No way. I couldn't stand the constant pressure. I'm fine where I am."

Frank sighed. "All right. Two weeks. And then you'll fly to Washington. Agreed." He hesitated a moment before glancing at her shyly. "Do you think you could stay a little while and visit with me *after* the meeting?"

"I'd love to. Thanks," she said, meaning more, much more.

"You're very welcome," he answered, then looked away. For the life of him, he couldn't recall the last time he had felt tears in his eyes.

The rest of the day was spent leisurely. They walked the shoreline of the island, talking about his doubts concerning her mother's career, and Hope was amazed to find out how proud he had been of her accomplishments. She had never realized how jealous he had become of her consuming passion for computers.

That afternoon she walked her father to the dock, her arm in his as they ambled toward the boat. "You've grown into quite a young lady, Hope. I'm very proud of you."

His words had been years in coming, but she blushed anyway. "Thank you for noticing."

"Oh, I've noticed before," he said with a twinkle in his eye. "I just never had the opportunity to say it until now."

"Opportunity?"

"All right," he admitted, sighing. "I guess I was too embarrassed to say anything because when you were near I was so busy trying to make up for my absences in your life that I played parent to the hilt. But I love you very much. Even if I don't always show it the way I should."

She squeezed his arm affectionately. "I know, Frank," she said quietly. "I feel the same."

He stopped and faced her; her hand still rested on his forearm. "Then will you do me a big favor?"

She nodded, eyes widening as she wondered what she could possibly do for her father. Certainly he wouldn't ask her to leave the island early again!

"Would you consider calling me Dad?" he asked, a faint pink glow tingeing his cheeks.

Unable to get a sound past the giant lump in her throat, Hope threw her arms around her father's neck and hugged him fiercely.

"I take it that means yes?" he asked, pulling back and letting her see his tears.

"Yes, Dad," she said softly, the lump in her throat still there.

He kissed her cheeks. "Thanks, honey," he said, just as choked up as she. "I'd better get going or I'll miss my flight. But I'll see you in two weeks. Right?"

Her agreement was another hug. And then he was gone, but the closeness she had shared with him for the first time in many years remained, wrapping her securely and feeling very much like contentment. It was a start . . .

HOPE BENT a blade of grass under Armand's nose. He was lying on the sheet, arms under his head and his eyes closed. A smile seemed to be etched permanently on his lips, curling them ever so slightly at the corners. He looked like a small boy who had just gotten away with stealing some juicy, fresh, autumn apples. What he'd actually done was down two dozen oatmeal-and-raisin cookies.

"I have to go back to Duluth, you know," she said softly.

"I know. I can feel it."

She stared at him, startled. "What do you mean?"

He smiled, opening his eyes to look directly at her with love shining from them like the sun. "I have given this some thought, *chérie*, and the only way I can explain it to you is that the closer you get to the answer, the weaker I feel."

"Weak?" Her voice was hardly more than a whisper. Her heart stopped, her breath jammed in her throat.

Armand sat up, his leg brushing hers. "I should not have told you."

She cleared her throat. "I need to know these things." She stared at the curve of his jaw, longing to reach out and stroke the raspy whiskers. "When did this begin?"

"The day you returned from your last trip."

"I see. And when were you going to tell me?"

He tipped her chin up, his thumb gently caressing her parted lips. "You have had company since you returned, and I have not seen much of you."

His hand retreated, and she felt cold. She stared out across the brilliant blue lake. Tears which had no business being in her eyes threatened to fall. He touched her thigh, softly stroking the denim. "Hope. Look at me," he commanded.

Her eyes darted to his face, then to the tanned hand touching her leg.

"Because I need to know what has happened in my past and find some answers that will resolve this puzzle does not mean that I want to leave you, my sweet."

"Are you sure?"

He inclined his head. "I am sure. And what if I had wanted to be a part of Faith's life, what difference would that make? I am here. With you. I wish I could stay, but we both know better." His eyes showed his sorrow. "But if there is a way, I will find you again. I swear it."

She flew into his arms, tears streaming silently down her cheeks and onto his bare chest. It wasn't fair that she should love him, then lose him!

But right now he was here with her, and all she could do was make the best of it. All the lonely tomorrows would arrive soon enough.

10

THE PROFESSOR was at his desk, shuffling the papers strewn all over its large walnut surface. "I know it's here, my dear . . . ah, here it is." He glanced up, his eyes dancing with delight. That he thought her questions about the first settlers were more fun than a jigsaw puzzle was obvious. "You'll never guess what I found."

She smiled, but her heart began its erratic thumping again. His discovery was an item he thought would interest her. "I can't imagine. What is it?"

"Bella Haddington called me and told me that you had stopped by. She also mentioned that she had suggested you visit some of the historic homes in the area." He peered over his glasses. "Did you?"

"Well, no. Not yet," she apologized. "I was planning to do that on this trip, although I'm not sure what good it would do. They were all built a century after the traders that I was studying lived."

He leaned back, satisfied. "Forgive me, young lady, but most people would think that. However, Bella gave me food for thought, and I began a little investigation of my own. One of the homes, the Picard home, just might belong to the great-grandson of one of the men you're looking for." He glanced at his notes. "The gentleman called Jacques Pillon. Many names changed in those times, because there were so many nationalities and each one had a different pronunciation and spelling.

"Occasionally a man would change his name to that of a distant, more wealthy branch of his family, as if by association, he, too, would become more wealthy or gain more influence over his own life and those around him. Especially then, when grand names and ties to the old country were such a status symbol. According to my notes, Pillon disappeared just before Picard came into his own business. Because of this, I believe they are the same man."

It took a few minutes for that information to sift through her brain. She stared at the older man, her mind stalled in first gear. Suddenly she stood, a bright smile on her lips. "The Picard House? Here in Duluth?"

He held out a slip of paper, and she reached for it with shaky fingers. "Yes. Here's the address. I wish you luck in your search. Meanwhile, if I find any other information, I'll forward it to your post-office box immediately."

Hope edged toward the door, almost too anxious to leave and see for herself. "You're sure?"

He bent his head to peer at her again. "I'm not sure. But if you want to be certain, going to the house might help."

Hope walked back and held out her hand, shaking his with a tight grip. "Thank you, Professor Richards. Thank you so very much. You've been terrific. Just terrific."

"Thank you, my dear," he said, looking at her as if she might be coming down with some mysterious ailment. "I wish everyone were as eager to find out more about their ancestors."

Hope laughed delightedly, and the professor took a step back. "Ancestors, yes. Oh, yes." Then she was gone, skipping down the steps and into her car.

She revved the engine, and with one more wave toward the professor's window, she was off. Suddenly she laughed again. The professor had been at the window rubbing the hand she had shaken. It would probably be a while before he had full use of it.

It took her an hour to find the right street, and by that time her enthusiasm had waned considerably. It was probably another dead end. After all, what did it matter that the house might belong to Pillon's ancestor? It was still a hundred years too late to be of any good to Armand.

The area had mansions sprouting on every corner. Sitting majestically among the older mansions, where millionaires had lived when the iron mines had created kings and money had flowed as abundantly as the water in Lake Superior, sat the Picard house.

A large wooden sign stood on the front lawn, proclaiming the John Picard Home, Hours from 11 to 5, Tuesday through Sunday, Closed on Monday. Not bad for a ragtag frontier scout's great-grandson. A glance at her watch told her it was half an hour before closing.

She tried the doorknob. The heavy oak door swung back easily on well-oiled hinges, revealing a bright entryway and a white vase with fresh flowers whose aroma almost overpowered her.

"Hello?" she called, but no one answered. "And a hearty welcome to you, too," she muttered to herself as she stepped over the threshold. Brochures about the house and a guest sign-in book lay on either side of the funereal floral arrangement. She picked up a brochure, and stuck her head inside the living room, just to the right of the foyer.

Occupying one side of the room was a Queen Anne table with a small grouping of chairs around it, as if it was a games table. A Victorian couch in petit point of reds and blues faced the fireplace. Two ottomans, also Queen Anne, perched between the couch and an over-stuffed chair.

Several other chairs were positioned around the room, and there were Victorian lamps with fringed shades on the small tables. The furnishings were certainly more recent than the earliest residents of the house.

The next room was set up as a bedroom with a lad-der-high four-poster bed taking up much of the space. There was also an ornately carved wardrobe, and a smaller chest with a pitcher-and-bowl lavatory on top.

She left the room, her heels tapping slightly on the patined wood floor. Next door was a study in which a huge wooden rolltop desk was the main attraction, with its pigeonholes empty except for a few brochures like the one Hope was holding. Against the wall was a—Hope finally glanced at the brochure—chaise longue made entirely of cigar-box mahogany. A rare treasure, indeed, and one that John Picard probably never owned.

She sighed. The exuberance she had felt since her talk with the professor seemed to drain from her slowly, leaving the hollow emptiness of disappointment behind.

As she turned to leave, her eye was caught by a framed shadow box on the side wall. Her heart began beating rapidly. Her breath stopped for a second. Her eyes had to be playing tricks on her. She blinked.

The carved frame was dark wood, while the shadow box itself was lined in leaf-green velvet, the front made of glass. In the exact center of the box, on the green velvet, lay a large—at least six inches long—intricately carved ivory key with a brass thread twisted around the stem to strengthen it. Under the frame was a small rectangular brass plaque that said the key had been given to John Picard's great-grandfather in the mid-1700s by a sea captain.

"My God, it really does exist," she breathed, her eyes glued to the key that Armand had spoken of so often. It was real.

She reached up, her fingers stroking the glass that blocked her from the object she hadn't really believed she would ever find.

A voice from behind her interrupted her reverie. "I'm sorry, but I didn't know anyone was here." Hope jerked back her hand as if it had been burned by the glass and turned to stare at the tall Victorian-costumed woman standing in the door. A smile touched the woman's lips, but her eyes were wary, carefully appraising the young woman who had been so brazen as to touch the antiques under her care.

"I called out, but no one answered." Hope tried to smile, but her lips wouldn't move.

The woman paused, looking pointedly at her watch. "Yes, well. Perhaps you could come back tomorrow. We're getting ready to close right now."

"Please, not yet!" Hope cried, suddenly galvanized into action. "I'll only be a moment. Please let me stay. I have to . . . oh, please, just give me a moment!" she cried as she sped down the hallway and out the door to her car. She fumbled with her keys, dropping them once before she unlocked the trunk and grabbed her camera. Then she was running back up the steps and into the study again, out of breath, but with such a brilliant gleam in her eyes that it seemed to startle the woman.

"Just let me get a picture and I'll go quietly. I promise," she said breathlessly, while the woman carefully worked her way backward out of the study and into the hall. Hope knew she had to be acting like a crazy woman, but she'd been doing that ever since she'd met Armand.

"I'm sorry, but I'm afraid—" the costumed woman began, but Hope interrupted.

"I know it seems crazy to you, but you see, my ancestor is the sea captain who gave John Picard that key, and I've traveled a long way just to see it. It will only take a minute to get a picture, then I'll go. I promise," Hope lied. But then someone else's lie had been put on a brass plaque under the key. What was the difference between their lie and hers?

The guide relaxed visibly in the face of Hope's stuttering lie. "Oh, well, in that case . . ." she began, but Hope ignored her as she set her camera and began shooting. She took fifteen or twenty shots before the woman finally began clearing her throat, implying that now her patience was really at an end.

Hope didn't remember getting back to the main street of the town, but the next thing she saw was a kiosk with a sign that proclaimed in large red letters that they would have pictures developed in one day or the cost of developing was free.

A plan was forming in her mind. She was acting more on instinct than logic, but she was going with it anyway. Logic be damned. She gave the film to the young man in the booth and received her receipt, then drove back to the hotel.

The key existed. It had been right under her nose all the time. Now all she had to do was steal it.

No, that wouldn't work. It was encased in what appeared to be a sealed shadow box, attached to the wall with four small brass screws. If she took it, the theft would be noticed right away and she'd be the first suspect, especially since she had just claimed the key as belonging to her family.

And she'd have to do it during the daytime, when the house was open. She had noticed that the windows had burglar alarms, which meant that as far as her bumbling theft was concerned, breaking and entering was out of the question.

Another idea hit. She'd exchange the key with one just like it. She didn't know how yet—she hadn't worked out the details. But that would work.

She wished Armand was with her so she could share the news with him. At word of this discovery, he'd probably fade even faster.

She slumped forward, feeling more frustrated than before. The buoyancy she had felt earlier ebbed to a new low. Again, intuition told her that with the discovery of the key came the loss of the man she loved almost more than life itself. She needed time to adjust, to think, to work out a course of action. She needed time to cry.

The next morning she bathed and dressed quickly. During the night she had formed a more concrete plan than that of the day before, and now it was time to implement it.

She drove to the photo store and picked up her film. There were fourteen usable shots in all, each capturing the key at a different angle. It really was a fine work of art. Armand must have paid a small fortune, even in his day, to have such a beautiful key crafted. First, she needed its exact measurements.

It took another hour for her to find a hardware store and complete her shopping. She bought a steel tape measure because it wouldn't stretch; she had to be sure of the measurements of the carved grooves, or cuts, on the blade of the key. She also found a screwdriver that looked as if it would fit the screws and still be small enough to hide in the palm of her hand.

Then it was back to the John Picard House.

Her knees knocked as she strode up the long sidewalk to the front door. She gave a silent sigh of relief when she realized the costumed girl who approached her was not the woman who had been there the day before. At least she didn't have to face two problems at once. Dealing with the key was enough for now.

She trailed through the rooms with the guide, the woman explaining in a singsong voice about the furnishings and the style of living the house had been built for. Hope forced herself not to give the key more than a cursory glance as she wandered from the study to the back bedroom. She nodded her head at the woman's explanations as if everything and nothing interested her, trying hard not to reveal her impatience.

At the end of the tour, where the donation cup was kept, Hope extracted a twenty-dollar bill from her wallet and smiled as she stuffed it in the cup, just deep enough to hold it but not enough to hide the denomination. The girl's eyes widened, as did her smile. "May I wander through by myself for a while? The house is so wonderful, I'd like time to take in everything you've shown me."

"Why, certainly. Make yourself at home, only please don't touch anything. It's all very old and fragile, and some of the vases and dishes have already been glued back together."

"I understand. I love old things, too," Hope said with an impish smile. Armand and ivory keys . . .

The guide waved her through. "Then be my guest. Normally I would be leaving in a hour, but I promised to take over one of the other girls' shifts today, so if you have any questions, just let me know."

Hope smiled and thanked her, purposely slowing her steps so the eagerness that flowed through her veins wouldn't show. She dallied in the back hall, pretending to study a second coatrack before making her way into the study. With a glance over her shoulder to ensure that she wasn't being watched, she pulled out the tape measure, and the pen and paper and began doing what she had come for. It took several minutes to line up the measurements, mostly because the key was hanging above Hope's eye level, and it was difficult for her to decide if her eyes could be trusted.

Voices echoed down the hallway. She quickly hid her tape measure and pad. Then she turned, and with a finger on her chin, she tapped her teeth as she studied the rolltop desk.

"Oh, are you still here?" the guide asked, apparently having forgotten about her.

Hope smiled, wishing she could draw breath. "Oh, yes. I was just studying that delightful desk. It's a wonderful piece, don't you think?"

The young woman nodded her head, then went into her singsong explanation for two elderly women. Hope waited until they wandered into the other room, letting out her breath as they did so. With a dexterity she didn't know she possessed, she flipped out the screwdriver and carefully undid one of the bottom screws that held the frame to the wall. It was hard work, because the screws had obviously been in place a long time.

By two-thirty that afternoon, she was standing at the front counter of a jewelry store, describing exactly what she wanted.

The owner scratched his wiry-haired scalp. "This isn't going to be easy, you know."

"Whatever it takes, I'll be more than happy to pay handsomely for your time and trouble. I'm sure you'll be able to do it."

He nodded. "I'll be able to do it as soon as I find a piece of ivory that big. Six inches isn't just floating around."

"Artists can get hold of it, so I know it's available," Hope protested. She'd take reticence from him, but she wouldn't take no for an answer. "Unless you'd rather I go to Minneapolis. I'm sure someone there could do it for me in just a few days."

He shook his head. "I can do it. I'll just have to send for the ivory."

"Then do it by express, please. I need this by next week." She took out the small screw she had taken from the original. "I also want it mounted in an identical frame, and the four corners must have screw holes this size."

"Yes, ma'am," he said wearily. His day obviously hadn't been the best.

In her car Hope leaned her head against the steering wheel and gave a huge sigh of relief. Now she could go home to Armand.

THE LITTLE MOTORBOAT was waiting patiently for her. As she climbed in and started the engine, her eyes searched the island. Somewhere at the top of the hill was Armand. From the other shore, the island appeared to be covered with trees, but she could just barely make out the boulder at the top of the hill. Soon the weather would change from summer to northern Minnesota's short-lived but breathtakingly beautiful autumn. The oak, maple and birch trees would turn vivid reds and yellows and sharp golden browns, then drop their foliage, exposing more of the island's secret hideaways to the naked eye. And she would be gone.

She couldn't see him along the shoreline. Cutting the engine, she threw the bowline over the piling, snubbed it and jumped out of the boat. One hand shielding her eyes, she looked up the path toward the top of the hill, but she didn't see him until she almost bumped into him. And when she did, her heart plummeted.

He was standing next to the small pine that marked the limits of his invisible wall. His doleful look stopped her in her tracks before another detail registered on her foggy brain. She could see the shrub he stood before. He was there, but only as a transparency of himself.

Her eyes glazed with tears. It was true. The closer she got to the key, the more he faded away. Her success was killing him.

"So you have decided to visit me?" His voice was soft as the breeze, but his tone was harsh and grating.

She moved toward him, stopping a few feet away. "You obviously know that I found out something. You wouldn't be disappearing in front of my eyes, otherwise."

He rubbed the back of his neck, ruffling his raven hair. She reached out to touch him, her fingers aching to soothe muscles that must have felt cramped. But she dropped her hand.

"Yes, my Hope. I know," he said resignedly, not noticing her futile gesture.

They walked the rest of the way to the top of the hill in silence. The end of their time together was near, and neither seemed willing to breach the wall they had erected to cover the pain that was certain to accompany their unbelievable loneliness.

Hope sat down on the blanket under the towering oak. Taking a breath, she came straight to the point. "I found the key. It's in a museum that used to be John Picard's house. He was the great-grandson of your scout, Jacques Pillon."

"I thought you must have." He continued to stand, his hands on his hips, staring across the water to the forest beyond, his eyes focused on the past. "So he was the one who probably killed me. Strange, but I would not have expected it to be him." He looked over his shoulder at Hope. "Did you get it?" He wanted to touch her, comfort her, but he did not know how.

She shook her head. "No. It's attached to the wall, and there are women who guard the place like watch-dogs." She twisted around and located her purse, to get one of the pictures she hadn't given to the jeweler. "I want to be sure this is it." She held out the photo, silently pleading with him to smile at her and make her load easier to bear.

He reached for it, but there was no smile. He gave the picture only a cursory glance before nodding his head. "Yes, that is the key."

"I thought so." Her tone was leaden.

He turned toward her, hands still on his hips, light still seeping through him. Strangely, it gave him a larger aura, making him appear even more powerful. "What do we do now?" he asked.

"*We* do nothing. I do." She turned to look at the view, only seeing Armand as she wished to see him: whole, complete and all hers. Slowly she swiveled her head and looked at his face. "I took the measurements and photos to a jeweler. He'll have a replica, right down to the frame, in about a week. I'll replace the original with a copy and bring the original back here."

He frowned. "But you said there were guards."

"There are, but I think I've found a way around that. All I can do is try."

"And then?" he prompted softly.

"Then I return here, and we fit the key in the chest. After that . . ." She shrugged, pretending it was all a matter of course. "We'll see."

The sun rose another notch as Hope stared into the bright day, trying desperately to curb tears that threatened to flow for all the wrong reasons. He wouldn't appreciate them, anyway.

She gasped as his hand tangled in the back of her hair, gently but firmly turning her to face him. "No, my Hope. That you will not do," he said softly. "Do you understand?"

"You're returning," she whispered, touching his cheek with her hand. He was becoming more solid with every passing moment.

"Yes," he answered. "But that was not what I was referring to. You will *not* do it. Do you understand?"

She raised her brows, pretending she didn't know what he was talking about. "Do what?"

"Take your own life." His answer was soft, but his words hit the air with the power of lit gunpowder.

She dropped her eyes. Even she had not been able to put the thought into words, but she knew that was what she wanted to do in order to be with him. "Why not?"

His dark blue eyes turned almost black with the need to make her understand. "Because it is not time for you to die. You have a long life ahead of you, with much in your future to look forward to." His hand tightened on her neck. "You may not believe me, but I know. I know this as certainly as I know that I love you with all my heart. I know as certainly as I know that your soul and mine will meet again, to conclude what our love has started."

The tears she had held at bay finally trickled down her cheeks. "You'll be leaving me, going to Faith, and I'll be left behind. Don't you understand? *I* love you more than she did! *I* want to spend my life—or death— with you!"

"And you will, but not by your own hand, and not until God calls you himself."

Anger welled up in her breast. She could barely breathe with the pressure of it. "Faith committed suicide at sixty-two! Do you know why? Because she realized she had made a mistake and wanted to be with you!"

He smiled sadly, his hand rubbing the curve of her neck again. "Poor Faith. She was not grown enough, not ready for love. Not even at sixty-two."

"You pompous ass!" she screamed, pounding his chest with her fists. "She died for you! Her with her childish love! Can I not do as well?"

He grabbed her fists, holding them to his chest and soothing the backs of her hands with his thumbs. "Yes. You can live, so I can complete my cycle and come back to you," he said softly. So softly she quieted.

She released her hand and rubbed at the tears on her cheeks, trying to make sense of his words. "I don't believe you," she said finally, staring at his chest because she was afraid to look into his eyes.

"I told you once before that I thought your soul was part of Faith's. The part that had to grow as a woman and as a human. I still believe that. I also believe we will meet again, or we would not be going through this time together. We are meant for each other." He smiled, lifting her chin so she could look at him and know how firm his conviction was. "I must believe that. And so must you."

Exhausted by the argument, she managed a wavering smile. "You're crazy. You know that."

His thumb wiped away an errant tear. "But I am not alone, Hope."

"No. You're not alone."

"Then you believe me?"

"I'm trying . . ."

He smiled, and this time his smile broke her heart. She would cradle the picture of it in her memory. It would have to last a long, long time . . .

"You will believe. And if you were right, my Hope, and suicide was the answer, would that not mean that Faith would be by my side right now?" He looked around, then brought his sharp gaze back to her. "If so, then where is she?"

"It didn't work." Her last hope was gone; she realized the truth of his words.

"So we will try my way instead, yes? I know it is the right way. I just know." He pulled her into his arms, turning her around so she could lean her back against his chest, leaving his hands free to cup her breasts as he gave a sigh.

"I love you," she whispered. "I love you so damn much it hurts."

"Then let me mend that hurt, Hope." His voice was midnight velvet in her ear, causing her breasts to fill with the same wanting his sultry voice had aroused.

"Yes," she murmured, flowing into his arms and wrapping her hands behind his head.

They made love with gentle abandon, then curled into each other's arms. Her lashes fluttered, then opened at last to stare into the indigo depths of his eyes. A different sort of lethargy had captured her body, a full, sated sensation that made her feel as if she had never known such completeness.

"Lie still, my Hope," he warned, and she did. He felt lighter than before. Then she realized why. He had exerted all his energy and was fading into the air.

A rock lodged in her chest. A bitter lump formed in her throat. His slow, devastatingly warm smile melted away the rocks and lumps. Nothing mattered except that he was with her. Now.

So she pretended everything was all right.

The days passed too quickly. Armand and Hope never left each other's side for long. The fear that he would disappear completely was never far from her thoughts, no matter how hard she tried not to show it.

Too soon the time came when she had to return to the jeweler's for the copy of the key. She didn't speak of it; she couldn't. But they both knew.

THE JEWELER was proud of his work, which was apparent to anyone looking at his smiling face. "Quite remarkable, isn't it?" he asked, holding it up for Hope's approval.

She studied the framed key, then the picture she had taken of the original. Nodding her head, she agreed. "You've done a wonderful job. It's perfect."

The jeweler carefully placed his work of art on the glass case in front of him, a frown creasing his forehead. "You know, one of the girls said she's seen this key somewhere."

"I bet she has." Hope smiled brightly. "The original is in the John Picard House. You see, my ancestor was the sea captain who gave it to Picard's great-grandfather, and since I couldn't have the original, I decided to have a replica made for my mother. She's so interested in the history of our family. It's sort of a birthday gift," she said, relying on the lie she had already given.

His frown disappeared. "What a nice thing to do. My mother is into all that family-history stuff, too." He laughed. "Though why, I'm not sure. We don't have any blue blood running through our veins. Just good old lumberjack stock."

Hope relaxed, the adrenaline dissipating as they broached a safer topic. She couldn't imagine how old his mother was, since he looked to be fifty or sixty himself. "Lumberjacks made this part of the world what it is today. That's just as important as our sea captain is to our family." She reached for her checkbook and wrote out the amount of the bill.

Fifteen minutes later she left the shop with the framed key under her arm. The jeweler had been a talker, and had posed questions that she'd had to dodge constantly. But now, with the precious item under her arm, she knew it had been worth it not to rush. Rushing would have made her look furtive or guilty, and then he might not have believed her explanation at all. He might even have questioned somebody at Picard House....

She stopped those thoughts, too busy with the next step of the plan to worry about how she had handled the last. Her muscles bunched with tension as she waited for someone to tap her on the shoulder and tell her she was breaking the law.

Once inside the car, she took the framed key and tucked it into a large canvas shoulder bag she had just purchased in a convenience store. It fit perfectly. Just before going to the jewelers, she had returned to the Picard home and loosened the two top screws, removing the second bottom one. Carefully lifting the screw from her coin purse, she tried it in one of the holes. It fit. Her sigh of relief filled the small car.

With nerves strung like tight wire, she pulled into a hamburger stand, ordered a grilled-cheese sandwich and a malt, then sat in the car while she ate it. In another hour, the Picard lady volunteers would change shifts, and another woman would work the late-afternoon period. Then she could stroll in and complete the job. With any luck at all, she'd be back on the island by this evening.

She had to be. That morning, Armand had been more ghostlike than she had ever imagined ghosts to be. He was an apparition, barely outlined against the blue sky or dark green of the trees. He couldn't disappear before she got back. He couldn't.

She had a hope, a dream that she had clung to these past several days. Perhaps if she did everything correctly and matched things the way they were supposed to be matched, the grateful Fates would allow Armand to remain, whole and free, to live with her.

It was time. Within minutes she was parked in front of the house, the screwdriver tucked in the back pocket of her jeans, a baggy sweater hiding the bulge it made. She grabbed her camera and the telescoping tripod and walked jauntily to the door. The gaudy canvas bag was heavy, but she acted as if it were the lightest thing on earth.

Her heart plummeted when she saw that the same stone-faced amazon from the first day was back. But her smile never wavered. "Hi, how are you," she called cheerily, waving the tripod as if it were a walking stick. "I'm here to take some pictures for one of the locals. He called and made arrangements, I believe."

The older woman never cracked a smile. "No one called," she said, her eyes narrowed suspiciously. "Which 'local' are you supposed to take pictures for?"

"Jeff Haddington. He wants them as a gift for his mother. Apparently she's into the history of Duluth, and he thought it would be a nice surprise. Besides, he thought his great-grandmother had a mahogany chaise longue just like this one, and knew his mother would appreciate an example of it. The photos are just for his own personal use, you understand. Mr. Haddington was supposed to make that clear to you." She stressed the name of the man who was becoming a pillar of Duluth society. He might as well serve some useful purpose.

The amazon's eyes lit up. Hope could imagine her giving her tour and dropping that little tidbit of information as if she had heard it from the great man personally. "Please go ahead. Do you need help?"

"No, thanks. My equipment takes a little time to set up, though," Hope babbled, moving toward the study at the back of the house. "The lighting, you know. It can be disturbed just by an extra shadow or a reflection."

Quickly she opened the tripod and attached her camera. Then it took five minutes to remove two stubborn screws from the original frame and slip the original key into her oversized purse. She had threaded the screws through the hole and had barely tightened one when the amazon appeared.

Hope's heart stopped, lodging in her throat. Her eyes darted to her purse to make sure the original was out of sight before she smiled benignly at the woman. Then she turned back to the frame and began unscrewing the screw she had just tightened.

"What are you doing?" the woman demanded.

Hope turned surprised eyes toward her. "Why, I'm taking down the key to photograph it. It's too high, you see, and the lighting reflects off the glass. I'll have to photograph it on the rolltop desk to do it justice."

"I'm afraid that's impossible," the woman's voice was sharp with disapproval. "Nothing is to be touched or moved. You might break the dustproof seal on the frame."

Hope shrugged her shoulders as if it didn't matter to her. "Okay, if that's the way you feel about it. I was just trying to get the best shot, that's all." She began tightening the screws again, praying her hands wouldn't shake. All four screws were in place and the camera aimed toward the frame before the woman left her alone.

As soon as she was gone, a giddy smile appeared on Hope's face. Her lungs filled completely for the first time since she had picked up the bogus key from the jewelers. It was all she could do not to dash out of the house and never look back.

As it was, after she calmed down, she spent another five minutes taking pictures. Then, equipment in hand and the original frame safely tucked away in her purse, she made her way down the hallway and out the door, expecting a large hand to clamp on her shoulder at any minute.

She giggled with relief as she drove away. Hope Langston, all-around photographer and mistress of intrigue.

She couldn't wait to get back and tell Armand all about it! Suddenly her smile disappeared, and her foot pushed harder on the gas pedal. She prayed she'd see him one more time.

Just one more time . . .

DARK CLOUDS boiled on the horizon, turning the tops of pines and aspens an ominous, smoky black. She noticed none of it. All her worries centered on Armand. Would he be there, or had he disappeared already—perhaps when she had screwed the last screw in place? Or was he waiting for her, the walls finally disintegrating? Her lips moved in another prayer as she began the trek up the small hill toward the rock—and Armand.

Her eyes darted continually through the trees, seeking the invisible wall, searching for him. Panic sent her feet flying. Her eyes scoured the underbrush, the forest.

"Armand!" she called, her voice echoing through the trees and across the lake. "Armand!" But he didn't answer, and her heart thudded painfully. Still, she kept going. When she reached their clearing, she dropped her purse and slowly did a complete turn, searching intently. Then, as her muscles finally lost their strength, she sank to the ground, leaning against the big boulder.

"He's gone." She heard herself say the words aloud, but her brain was too numb for them to register. She clung to only one thought.

She had to get him back. She had to! Just one last time, so she could tell him how much she loved him, feel at one with him again. He had been right all along, they were meant to be together. He was her other half. Her eyes burned at the futile thought of lost moments when she might have spoken to him. She had never told him about the feelings that went beyond her love—he was her necessity, as much as the earth, air, water, food.

The chest! She jumped to her feet and moved quickly toward the tent. The chest! The key and the chest had not been together yet! It still might work, might make him real instead of dissolving him! There *was* a chance . . . With strength she didn't know she had, she grasped the brass handle and pulled the chest out of the tent, dragging it toward the rock. Her breath was like a small bellows in her ears.

She ran back for the screwdriver and began picking at the dried earth jammed into the keyhole. Salty tears of frustration poured down her cheeks. Her moan turned into a cry at the earth's reluctance to give its prize away.

With determination born of desperation, she finally managed to break up the dirt enough to blow it out. She swiped at her chin, wiping away teardrops that had collected there and leaving behind a wide streak of dirt. She didn't care. Nothing mattered except the ancient brass chest that sat on the ground in front of her.

Scrambling across the ground, she reached for her purse and the framed key inside. She lifted it out, and at first tried to pry open the back of the sturdy frame. It wouldn't budge. Tiny mewling sounds rose in her throat. Finally, clutching a small rock in her shaking fingers, she smashed the glass and grabbed the key, cutting her hand in the process. She stared at the drops of blood for a moment. It didn't matter. There was no pain. Only the pain deep within her breast.

With another gulp of air, she slipped the key into the lock, working out the rest of the soil that had settled there over time. She had to be gentle, for fear of damaging the key or the lock. Her fingers shook with the delicacy of her task. If the key broke, any chance she had of getting Armand back would be broken, too. Tears continued to course down her cheeks. Though a gust of wind touched the wetness, she didn't feel it. She didn't know she was crying.

When she first heard the whistling, she thought it was the gathering wind playing a trick on her. But there it was again, soft and sweet, and as achingly familiar as it had always been. She froze, not moving a muscle as the minutes ticked by.

"Armand?" she whispered huskily, still unsure. She sniffled again, waiting for the tune to fade away. But it didn't. Instead it lilted on the breeze and wrapped around her, its haunting melody both treasured and feared. Was it a beginning or an end? "Armand? Are you here?" she asked the breeze again.

"Yes, *ma petite chérie*." His voice was whisper-soft, seeming to echo in her mind more than on the breeze, but filled with his own special blend of humor and sadness. "But I am afraid that I can see you far better than you can see me."

She twirled around, her eyes darting everywhere as she hoped against hope. "Where are you?" she whispered, suddenly afraid she was losing her mind.

"I am in the air, above you, next to you, my Hope."

"I found the key." She held it up in the air, like a sacrifice to appease the gods. She would give up anything to have Armand. Anything. "I put it in the lock, Armand." She tried desperately to gulp the lump from her throat. It hurt to breathe, hurt to see. Everything hurt so badly. A thousand knives slashed her skin and broke her bones, splitting her apart. She wiped away more tears with her sleeve. "I thought maybe you'd return if I used the key. But I'm too late."

"No." His voice reached out to her on a gust of warm air. "You are not too late, sweet. You are just in time."

"What should I do?" Although her voice was a bare whisper, it sounded like a child's cry in the night.

"Stand up, my *églantier*. Let me see you. All of you, just as when we met."

Her knees wobbled as she stood, but her hands were swift and sure as she undressed and turned around. She didn't care that she couldn't see him, as long as he was with her. Still with her. Talking to her. She couldn't lose this last thread that still tied them together. She wouldn't.

The warm breeze caressed her as if his hands were there, touching her breasts, teasing her stomach, soothing her skin with the warmth of his.

"I love you, my Hope. I love you more than I can say. But I do not have to explain that to you, do I? You understand, do you not?"

Her earlier fears had been groundless. There was no need for explanations now. He understood the depth of their love as well as she. Words weren't needed. "Yes. I know. And you know you are my life," she said simply. She stood straighter, dignity etched in every line of her naked form.

"Be strong, my Hope. Be as strong as you have it in you to be. We will meet again. No matter how or where, we will be together again. I swear this. And when next we meet, we will both be free to love and be loved. As it was meant to be."

Her heart was pounding, and she was filled with the abject fear of losing him. Yet she knew there was nothing more she could do. If he didn't stay, she would be empty, left with an unbearably lonely life held together only by memories. Unless he was right . . . "How . . . how do you know?"

He chuckled ruefully. "How do I know that the sun will rise again and again? How do I know that you will have fine children? There is certainty in both things. I just know."

Her stark fear turned to frustrated fury, building up inside her then bursting forth to release the unbearable tension she felt. "You're one hell of an arrogant, pompous Frenchman!" she screamed, wanting, needing, craving reassurance she knew he could not give her.

"And you are a very giving, loving woman with a temper that rivals the Furies themselves," he whispered in her ears, a hint of impish deviltry in his soft voice. "You are my sweetbriar."

Tears blurred her vision. She thrashed the air for his form, her arms raised high. "Don't go. Please don't leave me," she begged in a husky whisper.

"Shhh, little one. Let me feel you next to me one last time," he said. The breeze ruffled her long hair as she stood silent, finally closing her eyes to shut out the inevitable. Suddenly the warm breeze surrounded her, touching her here, there, wrapping around her waist as if it were her lover's arms. All the while her tears cascaded down her cheeks. Her breath came harshly, and so shallowly that it made her dizzy.

And the yearning built.

Wherever the breeze touched her, it fanned a fire that before only Armand had been able to build. It played with the loose strands of her hair, lit on her eyes and mouth, gently stroked her breasts and made them full and ripe with Armand's love.

A deep moan escaped her throat, but she couldn't say whether it was from the torture of losing him or the torture of the loving breeze.

"I love you, Hope. Never doubt it," the wind said, echoing the sound of Armand's voice in her mind.

She could only sigh in response. She tossed her head back and lifted her face to the sky, her hair swirling madly around her.

"No matter how or where, we will be together again. I swear it, my Hope. God is merciful, and we have suffered enough."

She shuddered then, losing her balance to the climax that electrified her body. But the wind wrapped tightly around her, holding her upright. A light puff once more touched her parted lips and she drank it in. Crackling lightning rent the air zigzagging across the sky before it burrowed back into a dark and ominous cloud and was gone.

She sank to the ground, head back and arms reaching toward the sky. A deep, tormented scream of denial ripped from her throat into the now-empty air, as if unbearable pain was tearing her very soul apart. "Noooo!"

She had to try! She had to bring him back! She scrambled on hands and knees toward the chest, quickly turned the key to spring the lock. The moment she did, the island fell silent. Not even a bird chirped.

He was gone.

THE NEXT THREE DAYS were a complete blur to Hope, and she was thankful for that in an absentminded way. She marveled that, when she looked in the mirror, she saw the same person she had been seeing for years.

"She walks, she talks, she's almost human," she muttered to herself one day, the first words she had spoken aloud since that stormy afternoon in the clearing. Then she gave a hollow laugh that ended with a sob.

Her mind had been put on hold. Every action she performed was only to enable her to exist until the next day. Nothing was important. Nothing mattered. *Nothing* was a word that described the sum total of her life. Without Armand's living presence, she had no life.

The months spent with him felt like a lifetime. Yet all she had to show for her love was a corroded brass chest and its contents: a diary written in French and a miniature of a woman who looked so much like herself that it was mesmerizing. Oh, yes. And an ivory key she carried strung around her neck like a talisman as a reminder of his deep love, his caring. His very existence. And every time she cried great sobbing cries, she held the key close to her breast and felt, if not a measure of peace, at least some comfort. Armand had once held it in his hands.

Sometimes she treasured the key. Other times she wanted to crush it, to damage it beyond repair, so that she could release herself from its hold on her. She wavered back and forth, but her love for Armand always won over her hatred of the Fates.

The fourth day she woke up angry. She sat up in bed and looked down at herself. For the past three days she had worn nothing but an old T-shirt and a pair of bikini panties. Both had seen better days. Her hair was oily and matted, her face puffy from crying, and there were smudgy bags under her blank, dull eyes.

"Damn you, Armand!" she screamed brokenly. "You left me! You left me behind, and now you have peace while I have nothing! Nothing! Do you hear me?" she bellowed, and it felt good. "Damn you! If you were any kind of a man at all, you'd have found a way out of this mess!"

Her fists pounded the mattress as she sat there, glaring at the ceiling. How *dare* he leave her behind while he floated around on some cushy damn cloud, or whatever souls did? Who did he think he was, giving her a taste of heaven only to leave her in a hell like this?

Then she began to laugh. Not only had he reduced her to a driveling idiot, she had let him! Well, no more, her mind cried. No more! She might be down, but she certainly wasn't out for the count. He could rot in hell before she'd waste one more day wishing for him!

Her body craved action. Any movement to feel alive once more. She packed her bag with enough clothes for a week. The key came off her neck for the first time and was tucked safely in her purse. Then, locking the door behind her, she headed for Duluth and, from there, Washington. She would see her father, testify before the Foreign Affairs Committee and then return to the island to pack her things.

On the way to the airport, she left Armand's diary with a translator. She instructed him to work backward, last page first. She would pick up as many pages as he'd completed within the next week. But she had a few other errands to do before heading for Washington.

She had her hair cut to a shorter, more manageable style, had her nails done, and even treated herself to a facial. The purple smudges under her eyes were still there, but her eyes themselves were gradually taking on a glittery hardness she wouldn't have thought possible a few months ago. Not even the jungles of Sao Jimenez had been able to do this to her! Everything in her life— her father, the kidnapping, her career—had been put into perspective by her experience with Armand.

But she couldn't resist the enormous power of the John Picard House. With plodding steps, she walked through the door and down the hall to see the ivory key once more. It was still there, the brass gleaming, the green velvet still lush. A small, sad smile touched her lips for the first time in more than a week, revealing the depth and vulnerability that nothing, not even time, could ever erase.

"Can I help you with anything?" Hope turned toward a young girl in Victorian dress standing hesitantly in the doorway.

"No, thank you. I'm just saying goodbye." Hope's smile was fleeting. One more quick look over her shoulder at the imposter key, and then she was gone, her heels clicking on the hardwood floor with a ghostly echo down the silent hallway.

IT WAS A LITTLE OVER A WEEK before she went back to Duluth. There was a newfound peace between Hope and her father. They had been able to communicate better than at any other time she could recall, and that brought a certain peace inside herself. At last.

But still her every thought, her every action recalled Armand. If she had ever thought her heart broken with his leaving, she was wrong. It was her day-to-day life, no matter where she was, that brought to mind her loneliness and his love. She missed him with every look she saw lovers exchange, with every breath of air that failed to satisfy the yearning so deep inside her.

And she couldn't talk about it, couldn't tell anyone. If she did, who would believe she was sane? Certainly not her father. So she just went on smiling at people she didn't know and didn't care about, carrying on inane conversations on subjects she had no interest in, and went on pretending she was fine. All the while she was bleeding inside. She had a wound that could not be fixed, patched, mended or cured.

When she left Washington, she promised her father she'd return in a month to spend the winter with him. She tried to reassure him she'd be all right, but both knew that was a lie. She could see his concern for her in his eyes, yet there was nothing she could do to relieve it.

Returning to Duluth and the island was even harder than staying in Washington. Hope drove onto the dock of Teardrop Island at five-thirty in the afternoon, the translated pages of Armand's diary tucked in her purse—unread. Night was falling more quickly now, and there was a briskness in the air that hadn't been there the previous week. Summer was over, and fall was looming. The leaves were beginning to dry, and at the first freeze they would display a glorious riot of colors.

That night Hope slept like a baby.

The next morning she showered, washed her hair and even applied a touch of makeup. Then, with the transcript of Armand's diary in her hand, she trudged up the hill to the boulder. That seemed a fitting place to read Armand's most secret thoughts.

Three hours later she was crying quietly. She had thought she had known him before, but she knew him even better now. The last passage he had written explained more than she had ever wanted to know.   *I do not know if Faith is capable of going against her father's wishes enough to be mine. She is still so young and so very frightened of the world around her. I pray that she will grow to trust her own judgment enough to be the woman I know she could be. But growing up is hard and requires the pain of learning wisdom. She has not grown above a young girl, and I wish her to be a full grown woman, ready to handle the problems that come to a wife and mother. I need her to be my equal partner in life, not my daughter or playmate. So far she seems to be dodging the pain of growth in favor of the pleasures . . . but I should not write so of my beloved. I, too, have faults that I must learn to live with and learn from. Only with Faith I am not sure that she even wants to learn. She seems to love the idea of loving me more than loving me for myself. Four nights from now will tell the tale. We will meet at midnight outside Port Huron. If she is there, then I will know that she is ready for the responsibility of marriage and all it entails. If she*

*is not, then I will also have an answer. I pray that her
answer and mine are the same all the rest of our lives.*

But it was the last line, written on a page all its own
by a shaky hand that reached out to her, touching her
with Armand's presence.   *No love ever remains the
same. With living comes growth. And if love does not
grow, it withers and dies. But the one ingredient love
must have most of all is hope. Nothing is worthy without it.*

Her mind exhausted, she set down the last page.
Tears filmed her eyes. When had he written that last
page? Before he died, or after he had left this earth?

One thing rang true. He had been right. Faith had
been too young to cope with a love that was both a thrill
and a threat to her.

There were so many parallels in Faith's life and hers.
Faith had lost her mother at an age when she needed
her, just as Hope had. Faith had wanted to fight against
her father's domination, but hadn't had the courage.
Hope had managed to escape and then come back and
make peace. But Faith had not. Even their birthdays
were within two days of each other. She wiped away a
tear. They had also loved the same man. Hope much
more than Faith, but then Hope was older and wiser.

She smiled at that thought. If that were the case, why
was she sitting here, still contemplating her love of a
ghost? Usually there were no second chances with
death. Once life was over, it was finished. Armand had
to be the exception to life after death, or ghosts would
have crowded the living off the earth!

Without Armand, her life would be lonely. But she
had things to do, even if she no longer had the one per-

son she had longed to share life with. She still had her job, a career that commanded respect even from the men of today. It wasn't everything, but it would have to be enough.

She had to go on. "But not here," she muttered. "Never again here." She stared at the scenery she had once loved so well. There wasn't a time in her life when she hadn't found peace in this majestic wilderness. Silver-leafed aspens, oaks bigger than houses, tall, skinny pines that waved gracefully at the deep blue skies. Fish that darted through clear waters, jumping with the pure joy of living. And her island, remote, yet on the verge of civilization.

She loved it all, but now it reminded her too much of what she had lost. There weren't any memories here that didn't contain some trace of Armand.

So it was back to this. Full circle. She had to have faith in Armand. He had said he would come back to her, somehow, some way. Someday. If that were true, then he could find her anywhere, not just here. He wasn't landlocked anymore.

Without looking back at the boulder, she walked down the path to the house and dropped the typewritten pages on the kitchen table, then headed toward the dock. She filled the tank with gas, then took off across the lake toward her car. She knew now what she had to do. When she reached the country restaurant, she pulled in and ordered lunch. Then she made a phone call.

"Mr. Haddington, please," she said with a thread of steel in her voice.

When he came on the line, she held her breath for a second, chiding herself for listening for Armand in every male voice. "Mr. Haddington, this is Hope Langston. I want to sell Teardrop Island, and I thought you might be interested in the listing," she said, getting right to the point.

"Oh, I am, Ms Langston. Very much." His voice was warm and reassuring. "When may I see it?"

"Whenever you like."

The line was silent for a moment. "If you don't mind the rush, I'll be by later this afternoon."

With a grim smile, she replied, "A little anxious, aren't you?"

He chuckled, and his tone surprised her. She closed her eyes suddenly.

"It's only because I've wanted to see the place for a long time. I was there once when your mother was alive, and I've thought about it ever since. As a matter of fact, I may even want to buy it for myself."

She vaguely remembered a tall, skinny boy staring at the hill, hands in his pockets, while his mother visited hers. The memory came and went, leaving no permanent impression. "Very well," she said quietly. "I'll see you this afternoon."

"By the way, Ms Langston. It was nice of you to uncover that piece of information about the cigar-box-mahogany chaise longue. Perhaps your mother should have named you Charity, since it was so charitable of you to pass along the information."

"I beg your pardon?" she asked, her mind a total blank. That dark, impish quality in his voice had closed out everything else.

"I believe you remarked that my ancestor might have had one exactly like it?" His tone still held a hint of devilish teasing.

The Picard House. She had told the women that Jeff Haddington thought his ancestors might have had a chaise like that one. "One never knows, Mr. Haddington," she said smoothly, for the first time permitting a small smile to tug at her lips. "One simply never knows."

"How right you are. I'm looking forward to hearing about your other finds. You certainly impressed the volunteer women at the Picard House."

"It wasn't hard," she quipped softly, earning a chuckle from him. "I'll see you later, then," she said before hanging up, the smile tilting her lips a bit higher. How ironic that Faith's descendant should be the one to buy an island that really belonged to Armand. Somehow it felt right.

THE TRIP back to the island was uneventful, except for dark, roiling clouds that appeared to be settling right over the island. Did this part of the country do nothing but thunder and lightning, or had all that begun only when Armand arrived on the scene? She couldn't remember such a stormy summer. She bit her lips in agitation. Lightning had given to her and taken away from her. If she never saw it again, it would be no loss.

For more than an hour she sat quietly in the living room, hands in her lap as she contemplated the summer that had just passed. Silently she was saying goodbye to the island. To Armand. Her eyes traveled to the open windows as the late-afternoon breeze gently ruffled the old-fashioned lace curtains.

Slowly the vacuum she had lived in since Armand's disappearance was beginning to lift. With each passing moment she was realizing how her perspective on life had altered.

She had been harshly tested in Central America, and she had survived. She had learned to adapt, to face each day and take what it had to offer. She had made it. Just as she would make it through this. Armand would have told her the same thing, she was sure.

She and her father stood a chance of beginning a new relationship. Not as father and daughter; it was too late for that. But as friend to friend.

Her thoughts leaped quickly back to the present at the far-off drone of a motorboat. She walked to the window, pushing aside the curtains just enough to catch a view of the small cove.

Jeff Haddington docked the rickety rental boat and tied it to the pier. He gave it a disdainful look that plainly said it could sink to the bottom for all he cared, and his expression made her grin. She watched him walk up the short path to the house, his broad shoulders back, his thick, dark hair windblown from the boat ride.

He looked so hauntingly familiar in some ways. She frowned, then forcibly shook off that feeling, but it wouldn't go away. Funny, but she felt closer to Armand right this moment than she had felt in the past week. She could almost hear his deep, husky laughter... And she could hear his words. *"No matter how or where, we will be together again. I swear it, my Hope.''*

She tensed, ready to bolt. Had she remembered the words, or had someone just whispered them in her ear?

From the dark cloud that had settled just over the island, a jagged bolt of lightning erupted and seemed to strike just behind the spot where Jeff Haddington stood. She jumped, her heart stopped, her breath caught in her lungs. Bile rose in her throat as she watched tensely, expecting him to drop to the ground, fried to a crisp. The hair at her nape was stiff from the electricity in the air.

Instead of falling, he merely glanced toward the sky and continued to walk up the path to her door, totally oblivious to the bolt that must have hit only inches behind him.

She stared, her eyes widening as she watched his long gait eat up the earth between them. Suddenly she smiled. Then she laughed joyously. Her feet were lighter than air as she ran toward the door.

He was whistling an old French lullaby. . . .

Sarah

MAURA SEGER

Sarah wanted desperately to escape the clutches of her cruel father.
Philip needed a mother for his son, a mistress for his plantation.
It was a marriage of convenience.
Then it happened. The love they had tried to deny suddenly became a
blissful reality... only to be challenged by life's hardships and brutal
misfortunes.

Available in AUGUST or reserve your copy for July shipping by sending your name, address, zip or
postal code along with a check or money order for $4.70 (includes 75¢ for postage and handling) pay-
able to Worldwide Library to:

In the U.S.	In Canada
Worldwide Library	Worldwide Libary
901 Fuhrmann Blvd.	P.O. Box 609
Box 1325	Fort Erie, Ontario
Buffalo, NY 14269-1325	L2A 5X3

Please specify book title with your order.

WORLDWIDE LIBRARY

SAR-1

Harlequin Temptation

COMING NEXT MONTH

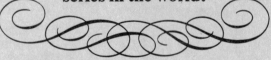